Parry walked up to the door of the apartment house, went in, and from his coat pocket he took the key that Fellsinger had given him. He opened the inner door.

In the elevator he wondered if Fellsinger had a cigarette holder up there. He was in great need of a cigarette. The elevator climbed four floors and came to a stop. Parry walked down the hall. He wished Fellsinger had some girl around. He had a feeling that falling asleep tonight would be hard work. He was at the door of Fellsinger's apartment and he put the key in the door and turned it and opened the door and went in.

Fellsinger was lying on the floor with his head caved in.

DARK PASSAGE

DAVID GOODIS

ZEBRA BOOKS
KENSINGTON PUBLISHING CORP.

ZEBRA BOOKS

are published by

Kensington Publishing Corp.
475 Park Avenue South
New York, NY 10016

First Zebra Books printing: July, 1988

Printed in the United States of America

TO MY BROTHER

CHAPTER 1

It was a tough break. Parry was innocent. On top of that he was a decent sort of guy who never bothered people and wanted to lead a quiet life. But there was too much on the other side and on his side of it there was practically nothing. The jury decided he was guilty. The judge handed him a life sentence and he was taken to San Quentin.

The trial had been big and even though it involved unimportant people it was in many respects sensational. Parry was thirty-one and he made thirty-five a week as a clerk in an investment security house in San Francisco. He had been unhappily married for sixteen months, according to the prosecution. And, according to the prosecution, a friend of the Parrys came into the small apartment one winter afternoon and found Mrs. Parry on the floor with her head caved in. According to the prosecution, Mrs. Parry was dying and just before she passed away she said Parry had banged her on the head with a heavy glass ash tray. The ash tray was resting near the body. Police found Parry's fingerprints on the ash tray.

That was half the story. The other half meant the finish of Parry. He had to admit a few things. He had to admit he hadn't been getting along with his wife. He had to

7

admit he was seeing other women. The fact that his wife was seeing other men didn't make any difference to the court. Then they got Parry to admit that he hadn't gone to work that day. A sinus headache kept him at home all morning and in the afternoon he had gone for a walk in the park. When he came home he found a crowd outside the apartment house and several police cars, the usual picture. That was what he said. The police said differently. The police said that Parry had hit his wife on the head with the ash tray and then arranged the body so that it would look as if she had tripped, knocking the ash tray off a table as she fell, then knocking her head on the ash tray when she reached the floor. The police said that it was a very clever job and no doubt it would have succeeded except for Mrs. Parry's dying statement.

Parry's lawyer tried hard but there was too much on the other side. There was only one weak link in the prosecution. It involved the fingerprints. When the prosecuting attorney claimed that Vincent Parry was a shrewd, devilish murderer, Parry's lawyer came back with the statement that a shrewd, devilish murderer would have wiped fingerprints from the ash tray. Parry's lawyer said it was no murder, it was an accident.

That was about all, except the character stuff. A lot of people wanted to know why Parry wasn't in uniform. The prosecution played that up big. Parry was a 4-F. The sinus was one reason, a bad kidney was another. Anyway he was a 4-F and added to that was something connected with a stretch in an Arizona reformatory when he was fifteen. He was an only child, an orphan, and his only relative in Maricopa said no and a week later he was hungry and robbing a general store. Then again there was this business of playing around with other women and there was a collection of statements from bartenders and liquor dealers. Parry had a habit of drinking straight gin despite the kidney trouble. The prosecution claimed that the gin was primary cause for the kidney trouble. Connecting the gin with the kidney, the prosecution made another connection and inferred that the 4-F status was attained through excessive gin that made the kidney worse. A few newspapers bit into that and began calling Parry a draft dodger. Other newspapers took it up. There were editorials calling for further examination of the 4-F's who complained of kidney trouble. When Parry was sentenced his picture was in all the papers and one of the papers captioned his picture "Draft Dodger Sentenced."

Just before he was taken to San Quentin, Parry got permission to talk to a friend. This was Fellsinger, who was a few years older than Parry and worked in the same investment security house. Fellsinger was Parry's best friend and one of the persons who believed Parry innocent. Parry gifted Fellsinger with all his possessions. These included a waterproof wrist watch, $63.75, a Packard-Bell phonograph-radio, a collection of phonograph records featuring Parry's assemblage of Count Basie specials and the late Mrs. Parry's assortment of Stravinsky and other moderns. Parry also handed over his clothes, but Fellsinger burned those and also got rid of everything that belonged to Mrs. Parry. Fellsinger was unmarried and he had spent most of his time with the Parrys. He had never liked Mrs. Parry and when he said good-by to Vincent Parry he broke down and cried like a baby.

Parry didn't cry. The last time he had cried was when he was in the reformatory in Arizona. A tall guard had punched him in the face, punched him again. When the guard punched him a third time, Parry went out of his head and put his hands around the guard's throat. The guard was dying and Parry was sobbing with tears as he increased pressure. Then other guards came running in to break it up. They put young Parry in solitary confinement.

Later on the brutal guard pulled another rotten trick on one of the kids and the superintendent investigated the situation and had the guard dismissed.

Parry was thinking about that as he entered the gates of San Quentin. He hoped he wouldn't run into any brutal guards. He had an idea that he might be able to extract some ounce of happiness out of prison life. He had always wanted happiness, the simple and ordinary kind. He had never wanted trouble.

He didn't look as if he could handle trouble. He was five seven and a hundred and forty-five, and it was the kind of build made for clerking in an investment security house. Then there was drab light-brown hair and drab dark-yellow eyes. The lips were the kind of lips not made for smiling. There was usually a cigarette between the lips. Parry had jumped at the job in the investment security house when he learned it was the kind of job where he could smoke all he pleased. He was a three-pack-a-day man.

In San Quentin he managed to get three packs a day. He worked as a bookkeeper and he made a financial arrangement with several non-smokers. He got along agreeably with other inmates and the first seven months were no hardship. In the eighth month he ran into the same sort of guard who had punched him during his Arizona confinement. The guard picked on him and finally arranged a situation where it was necessary to exert authority. Parry was willing to take the bawling out but he wasn't willing to take the punch. Then came the second punch. And on the third punch Parry started to sob, just as he had sobbed in Arizona. He put his hands around the guard's throat. Other guards came in on it and broke it up. Parry was placed in solitary.

He was in solitary for nine days. When he came out he was fired from the bookkeeping job and switched to another cell block, much less comfortable than the one he had been in. He learned that the guard had almost died and the episode had reached outside the prison walls and it had been in the papers. He was now doing hard work with a spade and a sledgehammer and at night he was practically out on his feet. He was almost too tired to read the letters he received from Fellsinger. But one night he got a letter from Fellsinger and it told him he was a sap for mixing with that guard. It ruined any chances he might have for a parole. He got a laugh out of that. He knew he was going to spend the rest of his life in this place. He knew what kind of life it was going to be.

It was going to be a horrible life. The food at San Quentin was decent but it wasn't good enough to get along with his condition. And somehow he had the paradoxical feeling that gin had helped his kidney and here he couldn't have gin. He couldn't have women and he couldn't have bright lights and he couldn't have a fireplace. He couldn't have the kind of friends he wanted and he couldn't have streets to walk on and crowds to see. All he had here were the bars on his cell door and the realization that he would be looking at those bars for the rest of his life.

He was sitting on the edge of his cot. He was looking at the bars of the cell door. Like a snake gliding into a pool a thought glided into his mind. He stood up. He walked to the door and put his hands against the steel bars. They weren't very thick but they were strong. He thought of how strong these bars were, how strong was the steel door at the end of corridor D, how ready was the guard's revolver at the end of corridor E, then the two guards at the end of corridor F, and how high the wall was, and how many machine guns were waiting there along the wall. The snake made a turn and started to glide out of the pool. Then it turned again and it began to expand. It was becoming a very big snake because Parry was thinking of the trucks

11

that brought barrels of cement into that part of the yard where they were building a storage house. Parry worked in that part of the yard.

Sleep was a blackboard and on the blackboard was a chalked plan of the yard. He kept tracing it over and over and when he got it straight he imagined a white X where he was going to be when the truck unloaded the barrels. The X moved when the empty barrels were placed back upon the truck. The X moved slowly and then disappeared into one of the barrels that was already in the truck.

The blackboard was all black. It stayed black until a whistle blew. The motor started. The sound of it pierced the side of the barrel and pierced Parry's brain. There wasn't much air but there was enough to keep him alive for a while. A little while. The sound of the motor was louder now. Then the truck was moving. He knew just how far it had to move until it would be out of the yard. He waited to hear the sound of a whistle. The sound of a siren. He had the feeling that this was nothing more than a foolish idea that would get him nowhere except back in solitary. He shrugged and told himself he had nothing to lose.

There was no whistle. There was no siren. The truck was going faster now. He couldn't believe it. This had been too easy. He told his mind to shut up, because this wasn't over yet. This was only the beginning and from here on it was going to be tough. He had to get out of the barrel and that was going to be a real picnic. He was in one of the bottom barrels and they were stacked three deep. The truck was rolling now. He sensed that it was making a turn. It made another turn and then it rolled faster. He was having trouble drawing air from the black inside of the barrel. He told himself that he had five minutes and no more. Two barrels on top of him, and four rows of barrels between him and the edge of the truck. He took a deep breath that wasn't so deep after all. That scared him. He took another

12

deep breath and that was less deep than the first. He threw his weight against the side of the barrel and the barrel wouldn't budge. He tried again and he made about an inch. He tried a third time and made another inch. He kept on trying and making inches. All at once it came to him that he was battling for his life. It scared him so much that he stopped trying and he decided to start yelling, to start begging them to stop the truck and let him out of the barrel.

Just before he opened his mouth he analyzed the idea. The gap at the top of the barrel was wide enough for his voice to get through, but if his voice got through it would mean that he would soon be back at San Quentin.

His mouth stayed open but did not release sound. Instead he made another drag at air. He pushed again at the side of the barrel. Now he estimated that three minutes were subtracted from the original five. He had two minutes in which to make good. He kept on dragging at air and pushing at the side of the barrel.

August heat came gushing through the gap at the top of the barrel, mixed with the black thickness in the barrel and the anguish and the effort. Perspiration gushed down Parry's face, formed ponds in his armpits. All at once he realized that more than two minutes had passed, considerably more. Put it at ten minutes. He looked up and through the gap at the top of the barrel he could see yellow sky. He smiled at the sky and now he understood that he had a good chance. Along with the sky a supply of new air was coming through the gap.

Heaving at the side of the barrel, pushing it away from the two barrels on top, he widened the gap to ten inches. He was working on the eleventh inch when the truck hit a bump in the road and the two barrels on top went sliding back to their previous position. He looked up and instead of yellow sky all he could see was black, the black underside of the second barrel. He had lost the gap and he had lost all the air. Now he must start all over again.

He didn't want to start all over again. He wanted to weep. He began to weep and the tears were thick spheres of wet mixing with the wet of increased perspiration. His cramped limbs were giving him pain. He measured the pain and knew that it was bad. And it would get worse, keep getting worse until finally it would blend with the pain in air-starved lungs. Once more he told himself that he was going to die here in the barrel.

Hate walked in and floated at the side of fear. Hate for the bump in the road that had caused the two barrels to slide back. Hate for the two barrels. Hate for the truck. Hate for the prosecuting attorney. Hate for Mrs. Parry. Hate for Mrs. Parry's friend who had entered the apartment that winter afternoon and found the body. Her name was Madge Rapf. Her name was Pest. She had been the Pest from the first moment Parry had known her. She was always in the apartment, butting in. Getting herself invited to dinner and staying late and trying to make time with Parry. Once she had made a certain amount of time with him and he remembered it was on a night when he and Mrs. Parry had engaged in a vicious quarrel. Mrs. Parry had gone into her room and slammed the door. Madge went into the room and stayed there for about twenty minutes. When she came out she asked Parry if he would take her home. He took her home and when she got him inside she started in on him. He didn't want to do anything. She didn't really attract him. She was nothing very special. But he was sick and tired of Mrs. Parry and he didn't particularly care what happened. So he began seeing her and one night it got to a certain point and then he told Madge to lay off, he was going home. She began to pester him. She told him that Mrs. Parry was bored with him but she wouldn't be bored with him. She told him he should

14

split with Mrs. Parry. He told her to mind her own business. But her nature made that impossible and every time she got the chance she told him to split with his wife and pitch in with her. She had been separated from her husband for six years and during all that time he had been trying to get a divorce. She wouldn't give Rapf a divorce because she knew every now and then he had another girl he wanted to marry. She had nobody. She had nothing except the hundred and fifty a month she got from her husband. Now the hundred and fifty a month didn't satisfy her and she wanted somebody. She was miserable and the only thing that eased her misery was to see other people miserable. If they weren't miserable she pestered them until they became miserable. Parry had a feeling that one of the happiest moments in Madge Rapf's life was when the foreman stood up and said that he was guilty.

It was getting awful in the barrel. Parry pushed the hate aside and replaced it with energy. He pushed at the side of the barrel. He made an inch. He made another inch and he had air again. The truck was traveling very fast and he wondered where it was going. He kept pushing at the side of the barrel. The truck hit another bump, hit a second bump, hit a third and a fourth. Parry figured there might be a fifth bump and he advised himself to be ready for it. The four bumps had pushed the two barrels back the way he wanted them to go back. He had about five inches up there. When the fifth bump came he was prepared for it and he heaved hard, going along with the bump, getting the two barrels over to the side, increasing the gap to what he measured as nine inches. He thrust his arms up, pushed at the two barrels, made four more inches. And that was plenty.

Parry pulled himself out of the barrel. He saw the road going away from him, a dark grey stream sliding back between level pale green meadow, sliding toward the yellow horizon. On the left, bordering the pale green, he could see shaggy hills, not too high. He decided to make the hills.

Keeping his head low he weaved his way through the barrels. Then he was at the edge of the truck, figuring its speed at about fifty. It was going to be a rough fall and probably he would get hurt. But if he fell facing the truck, running with the truck, he would be playing along with the momentum and that would be something of a benefit.

He did it that way. He was running before he reached the road. He made a few yards and then went down flat on his face. Knowing he was hurt but not knowing where and not caring, he picked himself up quickly and raced for the side of the road. The pale green grass was fairly high and he threw himself at it and rested there, breathing hard, too frightened to look at the road. But he could hear the truck motor going away from him and he knew that he was all right as far as the truck was concerned. When he raised his head from the grass he saw an automobile passing by. He saw the people in the automobile and their faces were turned toward him and he waited for the automobile to stop.

The automobile didn't stop. Parry stayed there another minute. Before he stood up he took off the grey shirt, the white undershirt. Stripped to the waist he felt the heat of the sun, the thick moisture of deep summer. It felt good. But something else felt bad and it was the pain in both arms, in the elbows. He had fallen on his elbows and the skin was ripped and there was considerable blood. He pulled at grass, kept digging at earth until there was something of a hole, a semblance of mud. He rubbed mud on his elbows and that stopped the blood and formed a protective cake. Then he put the shirt and the undershirt in the hole. He replaced the clods of grass, covering the hole smoothly.

The sun was high, and Parry watched it as he started toward the hills. He guessed the time as somewhere around eleven, and it meant he had been on the truck for almost an hour. It also meant San Quentin had taken a long time to discover his exit. Again he was telling himself it had been too easy and it couldn't last and then he heard the sound of motorcycles.

He threw himself at the grass, tried to insert himself in the ground. As yet he couldn't see the motorcycles, although his eyes made a wide sweep of the road. That was all right. Probably they couldn't see him either. They were coming around a gradual bend in the road. They made a lot of noise, a raging noise as they came nearer. Then he could see them, whizzing past. Two and three and five of them. Just as they passed him they began using sirens and he knew they were going after the truck.

He could picture it. The truck was say three miles down the road. Give them five minutes to search the barrels, to question the driver and helper. Give them another six minutes to come back here, because they would be going slowly, studying the road and the meadow at the sides of the road. All right, wait one more minute and let them make a mile and a third. Let it be two minutes, then take three or four minutes to get to those hills, and pray there wouldn't be any more motorcycles tearing down the road.

CHAPTER 2

When he was in the hills he sat down for a rest. He wondered if it would be feasible to stay here in the hills, give himself a few days here while the search radiated. But if the police couldn't get any leads elsewhere, they'd come back to the road and chances were they'd sift the hills. The more he thought about it the more he understood the necessity for keeping on the move. And moving fast. That was it. Fast. Everything fast.

He got up and started moving in the direction he had first taken. The hills seemed to move along with him. After a while he was tired again but he was thinking in terms of speed and he refused to take another rest. The weariness went away for a time but after some minutes it came back and it was accompanied by thirst and a desire for a cigarette. He couldn't do anything about the thirst but there was an almost empty pack of cigarettes in his trousers pocket. He put a cigarette between his lips and then he searched for a match. He didn't have a match. He looked around, as if he thought there might be a place where he could buy a book of matches. He puffed at the cigarette, trying to imagine that it was lit and he was drawing smoke. He didn't have any matches. He began to think of the things he didn't have.

He didn't have clothes. He didn't have money. He didn't have friends. No, he was wrong there. He had a few friends and one friend in particular. And it was a cinch that Fellsinger would go to bat for him. But Fellsinger was in Frisco and Frisco was going to be a very hot place aside from the heat of August. Nevertheless it was practical for him to see Fellsinger. The next move was Frisco. The police wouldn't watch Fellsinger. Or maybe they would. Or wouldn't.

As an hour passed the hills gave way to another stretch of pale green. There were no roads, there were no houses, nothing. Parry negotiated the pale green, moved toward dark green. It was heavily wooded area and he tried to guess what was on the other side. He looked back, knowing that the division of terrain would be a decent sort of guide, preventing him from traveling in a circle. He entered the woods.

He was in the woods for more than an hour. He was moving fast. Then he could see a lot of bright yellow breaking through the dark green. It meant that he was about to come out on the other side of the woods. Already he could see a band of white-yellow out there and he knew it was a road.

At the side of the road he leaned against a tree, waiting. He wanted to see a truck or an automobile and at the same time he was afraid to see anything of that sort. He kept sucking at the unlighted cigarette. He looked at the other side of the road and saw a continuation of the woods. All right, let an automobile come by. Let something happen.

Nothing happened for about forty minutes. Then Parry heard a sound coming down the road and it belonged to an automobile. There was an instant of animal fright and he was turning to dart back into the woods. A spurt of

.mbling spirit pushed aside the fright and Parry ran out to the center of the road. He saw the automobile coming toward him. It was a Nash, a 36 or 37, he wasn't sure but he didn't particularly care either. It was something that might take him to Frisco, if it was going to Frisco. He was out there in the center of the road, waving his arms beseechingly. The Nash was going rather fast and it didn't look as if it was going to stop. It increased speed as it closed in on Parry. There was only one person in the car and it was a man. It was a very pleasant man who was using this method to tell Parry that he would either get out of the way or get hit.

Parry got out of the way and the Nash went ripping down the road. Another fifteen minutes came in and went out again. Parry was leaning against the same tree. He wanted a match badly. He wanted water badly. He wanted a lift badly. He wished it wasn't August. He wished he had been born somewhere up in the Arctic Circle where these things didn't happen to a man. He heard another automobile.

This was a Studebaker. It was from way back. It was doing about thirty and Parry had an idea it couldn't do any more no matter how hard it tried. Again he was out in the center of the road, waving his arms.

The Studebaker stopped. Its only occupant was the driver, a man in old clothes, a man who looked Parry up and down and finally opened the door.

Parry stepped in. He closed the door and the man put the car in gear and got it up to thirty again. Parry had already noticed that the Studebaker was a coupé and the man was about forty or so and he was about five eight and he didn't weigh much. He wore a felt hat that had been dead for years.

For a few minutes there was no talk. Then the man half looked at Parry and said, "Where you going?"

"San Francisco."

The man looked at him directly. Parry looked straight ahead. He was thinking that approximately four hours had passed since he had stepped into the barrel. Perhaps by this time it was already in the papers. Perhaps the man had already seen a paper. Perhaps the man wasn't going to San Francisco. Perhaps anything.

"Whereabouts in Frisco?" the man said. He pushed the hat back an inch or so.

Parry was about to say Civic Center. Then he changed his mind. Then he took another look at the man and he came back to Civic Center. It really didn't make much difference what he said, because he was going to get rid of this man and he was going to take the car.

He said, "Civic Center."

"I'll get you there," the man said. "I'm taking Van Ness to Market. How come you're using this road?"

"Fellow gave me a lift. He said it was a short cut."

"How come he left you off back there?"

"We had an argument," Parry said.

"What about?"

"Politics."

"What are you?"

"Well," Parry said, "I'm non-partisan. But this fellow seemed to be against everything. He couldn't get me to agree with him and finally he stopped the car and told me to get out."

The man looked at Parry's bare ribs. The man said, "What did he do—steal your shirt?"

"No, I always dress this way in summer. I like to be comfortable. You got a match?"

The man fished in a coat pocket and two fingers came out holding a book of matches.

"Want a cigarette?" Parry said as he scratched a match.

"I don't smoke. Mighty funny looking pants you got

21

e."

"I know. But they're comfortable."

"You like to be comfortable," the man said, and then he laughed, and he kept on looking at the grey cotton pants.

"Yes," Parry said. "I like to be comfortable."

"You can keep the matches," the man said. He kept on looking at the grey cotton pants. He dragged the Studebaker back to twenty-five, then to twenty. His eyes went down to Parry's heavy shoes.

Parry said, "How come you got matches if you don't smoke?"

The man didn't answer. Parry kept his face frontward but his gaze was sideways and he could see the man's weather-darkened features and the short thin nose and the long chin. He got his gaze a little more to the side and he could see the car and the mixture of black and white hair beneath the rippling brim of the felt hat. The right temple, he was thinking. Or maybe just under the right ear. He had heard somewhere that just under the ear was the best place.

"Where you from?" the man said.

"Arizona."

"Whereabouts in Arizona?"

"Maricopa," Parry said truthfully.

"Hitched all the way from Maricopa, eh?"

"That's right," Parry said. He eyed the rear-view mirror. The road back there was empty. He got ready. His right hand formed a fist and he tightened it, making it hard. His right arm quivered.

The man said, "Why Frisco?"

"What?"

"I said why are you going to Frisco?"

Parry rubbed his fist against his thigh. He turned his body and leaned against the door as he looked at the man. He said, "Mister, you get on my nerves with all these

22

questions. I don't need to be bothered with you. I can get another ride."

The man frowned, deepened it and then let it break and shape itself into a weak grin. He said, "What you getting excited about? All I did was—"

"Forget it," Parry said angrily. "I'll pick up the kind of a ride where I don't have to tell my life history. How far am I from Frisco?"

"No more than fifteen miles," the man said. "But you're being foolish. I'm trying to help you out and you're—"

"Stop the car, mister. And thanks for taking me this far."

The man shrugged. He lifted a foot from the accelerator, brought it over to the brake. The car moved to the side of the road and as it came to a stop Parry leaned forward and sent his right arm toward the man's head. His fist landed on the upper part of the man's jaw, just under the ear. The aim was all right, but Parry didn't have much of a punch and the man let out a yell and clutched Parry's arm as the fist went forward again. Parry squirmed and tried to use his left. The man was stronger than Parry had supposed, and mingled fear and desperation increased the strength and tripled Parry's trouble. The man brought up a knee and tried to put it against Parry's groin. Parry managed to send a straight left into the man's face and the man let out another yell. The knee made another try at Parry's groin. Parry tried to stand up, but the knee was in his way. The man began to shout for help. Parry put another left in the man's face, followed it with a straight right that landed against the man's temple. The man was all fear now and he stopped shouting and he began to plead. As Parry hit him again he begged Parry to lay off. He said he didn't have much money on him but he'd hand it over if Parry would only leave him alone and allow him to go on his way. Parry again banged him on the temple, banged him on the jaw and on the temple again. The man's head went back and

Parry punched him under the right ear and knocked him out.

Parry was very tired. He blew air out of his mouth and rested his head back against torn upholstery. Through the sound of the idling Studebaker he could hear another sound, the sound of an automobile coming down the road. It was coming from the Frisco direction. Straight ahead down the road it was a shining grey convertible coupé that was growing too quickly. Parry wanted to throw the whole thing away. He wanted to open the door and leap out into the woods and keep going. He called that a bright idea and told himself that another bright idea was to try hiding on the floor of the Studebaker. They were wonderful, these bright ideas. He saw smoke coming up from the floor, coming from the half-smoked cigarette. He reached down, picked up the cigarette, brought it toward the face of the unconscious man. He had his hands cupped around the end of the cigarette. He had his eyes on the grey convertible coupé coming down the road. Let them think there had been three in the Studebaker and the Studebaker was stopping here so that one of them could go into the woods for something and the other two were waiting here and having a smoke.

The grey convertible rushed in and went past. Parry blew more air out of his mouth. There would soon be another car coming down the road. Now the road seemed to average a car every four or five minutes. Let the next car think there was only one in the Studebaker, and the Studebaker was parked here while the driver went into the woods for something. Parry opened the door, pulled the unconscious man out of the car and quickly dragged him into the woods. he undressed the man and he was putting on the man's clothes when the man opened his eyes and started to open a bleeding mouth. Parry bent low and chopped a right to the side of the head. The man went out again and Parry went back to his dressing.

It wasn't a bad fit. The felt hat was the best item. It had a fairly wide brim that would shadow his face to a great extent. There was a dirty checkered shirt and a purple tie with orange circles on it. There was a dark-brown coat patched in half a dozen places and a pair of navy-blue trousers rounding out their first decade.

He had the clothes on and he was going back to the Studebaker. Nearing the edge of the woods he stopped and put fingers to his chin. He saw the Studebaker and the grey convertible coupé parked directly behind the Studebaker. The grey convertible was a Pontiac. He saw grey-violet behind the wheel. Grey-violet of a blouse belonging to a girl with blonde hair. She was sitting there behind the wheel, waiting for Parry to come out of the woods. He decided to go back into the woods and keep on going. As he turned, he saw the girl open the door and step out of the Pontiac.

She saw him. She beckoned to him. There was authority in the beckoning and Parry was very frightened. He completed the turn and he started to run.

It was hard going. There were a lot of trees and twigs in his way. He could hear footsteps back there, the breaking of foliage, and he knew the girl was coming after him. Once he looked back and he saw her. She was about twenty yards behind him and she was doing her best. The snake came gliding into the pool. He would get her about fifty yards deep in the woods and then he would knock her unconscious and go back and grab the Studebaker. The snake made a turn and started gliding out of the pool. He didn't need to knock her unconscious. He didn't need to be afraid. The whole thing was very simple. The girl was lost on the road. Her Pontiac had passed the Studebaker and gone down the road maybe a half mile and when she saw she was lost she made a U-turn. She remembered the parked Studebaker and she came back to ask directions. That was all. He had only imagined the authority in tnat beckoning. It was curiosity and perhaps a stubborn decision to get her bearings that made her chase him through the woods.

Anyway he was now fifty yards deep in the woods and either way there was nothing to worry about. He stopped and turned and waited for her.

She came running up to him. The grey-violet blouse was supplemented by a dark grey-violet skirt. She was little. She was about five two and not more than a hundred. The blonde hair was very blonde but it wasn't peroxide. And there was a minimum of paint. A trace of orange-ish lipstick that went nicely with genuine grey eyes. She was something just a bit deeper than pretty, although she couldn't be called pretty. Her face was too thin.

He said, "What's on your mind?"

"I had a look at the fuel gauge. It shows almost empty." Her voice harmonized with the grey eyes and the lack of peroxide in her hair.

Parry said, "Where do I come in?"

"I don't know this road. I'd hate to be stuck here."

"So would I." Parry examined the grey eyes and couldn't find anything.

She was looking at the old clothes. She said, "Could you spare a few gallons? I'd pay a dollar a gallon."

It was an equation and it checked. The thing to do was to get rid of her in a hurry. Parry said, "Let's go back to the road and we'll talk it over."

They started back to the road. Parry waited for something but it didn't happen. He guided her away from the spot where he had left his man, and yet he had a feeling that she had already seen the man. He had a feeling that the gasoline story was just a story. Maybe this girl was lonely and she wanted a friend. Maybe this girl was

26

starved for excitement and she wanted action. There were a lot of maybes and none of them went anywhere.

He got another good look at her. She was twenty-seven if she was a day. Give her a big break and call her twenty-six. He saw lines under her eyes that told him she didn't get much sleep. The way her lips were set told him she didn't get much out of life. One thing, she had money. That grey-violet outfit was money. The Pontiac was money. He looked for something on her hands and the only thing he saw was a large pale amethyst on the ring finger of her right hand.

They came to the edge of the road. She turned to him and said, "All right, let's get in my car and get out of here fast."

CHAPTER 3

Parry took a step away from her. He said, "I don't get you."

She gestured back to the woods. "I saw the body."

"He isn't dead. He gave me a lift and he tried to take my wallet. I knocked him out and then I got scared and took him into the woods. I'm not scared now. I'm going to take his car. Don't you try to scare me."

"I'm not trying to scare you," she said. "I'm trying to help you." She started toward the Pontiac and gestured for him to come along. She said, "Come on, Vincent."

He stood there with his eyes coming out of his face.

She said, "Please Vincent—we don't have much time."

He stabbed a glance at the idling Studebaker. Then he remembered that the Studebaker couldn't do better than thirty. The Pontiac could do plenty. It was a 1940 and it had good tires. He could use something like that. He looked at the girl. He looked at the point of her chin.

He took a step toward her.

She didn't budge. She said, "It won't get you anywhere, Vincent. If you're alone in that car you'll be picked up. If you come with me I'll hide you in the back seat. I've got a blanket there."

"You're with the police."

"If I was with the police I'd be carrying a gun. Look, Vincent, you've got a chance here, and if you don't take it—"

"I'm going to take it." He took another step toward her. This time she cowered. Backing away from him she pleaded, "Don't do it, Vincent. Please don't. I'm for you. I've always been for you—"

It stopped him. He said, "What do you mean—always?"

"From the very beginning. From the day the trial opened. Come on, Vincent—please? Stick with me and I won't let them get you."

The way she said it brought tears to his eyes and out of his eyes, brought the thought from his brain and out of his mouth and he said, "I don't know what to do—I don't know what to do—"

She put a hand on his wrist and took him to the Pontiac. She opened the door, pulled up the front seat. He got in the back and crawled under the blanket.

The door slammed. The motor started and the Pontiac began to roll.

He got his head out from under the blanket and he said, "Where are we going—Frisco?"

"Yes. You'll stay at my place. Keep under that blanket. We're due to be stopped. They've got all roads blocked. We're lucky they're not probing this road."

"You're in on it. I know you're in on it." He couldn't get the quiver out of his voice. The tears kept coming out of his eyes.

The Pontiac was doing forty. It made a turn and Parry felt a sudden decrease in speed. Then he heard the sound of motors—sharp little motors—motorcycles. His body started to shake. He tried to stop the shaking. He bit deep into the back of his hand. The motorcycles were coming from up front, closing in, getting louder. The Pontiac went down to twenty—fifteen—it was going to stop.

He could hear her saying, "Don't move, Vincent. Don't make a sound. It's going to be all right."

The Pontiac stopped. The sound of motorcycles came close, broke like big waves nearing a beach, then became little waves coming up on the beach. The motorcycles were idling now. Parry pictured them parked at the side of the road. All he could see was the black inside of the blanket that was even blacker than the inside of the barrel. And yet he got his mind past the blanket and he could picture the police walking over to the parked Pontiac.

Then he didn't need to picture it any more because he was hearing it.

A motorcycle policeman said, "Got your license, miss?"

He could hear the sound of a panel compartment getting opened. He begged himself to stop the shaking.

"Where are you going, miss?" The same voice.

"San Francisco."

"I see you live there." The same voice.

"Yes." It was her voice. "What's the matter, officer? Have I done something wrong?"

"I don't know yet, miss." The same voice.

Then another voice. "Carrying anything?"

Then her voice again. "Yes."

"What have you got?" The first voice. "What have you got there in the back!"

Her voice. "Old clothes. I'm making a collection for China War Relief."

The first voice. "We'll have a look, if you don't mind."

Her voice. "Go right ahead."

The sound of the door opening. The sound of the blonde girl moving over so that the policemen could gain access to the back seat. He started to picture it again. They were looking at the blanket. They were going to lift the blanket. Then he could feel it—their fingers touching the blanket, lifting the edge of the blanket. He pulled his hand

30

inside the sleeve of Studebaker's coat. They could see the sleeve now, but they couldn't see his hand. And they could see part of the coat and that was as far as they got. They took their fingers away from the blanket.

The first voice. "Well, I guess it's all right, miss. Sorry to have troubled you, but we're checking every car on this road."

Her voice. "Perfectly all right, officer. Will there be anything else?"

"No. You can drive on now."

The sound of the door closing. The sound of the motor rising. The Pontiac rolled again. Parry felt a wetness against his lips and it was blood coming thickly from the back of his hand, getting through the place where his teeth had penetrated the sleeve.

The Pontiac made a turn. It picked up speed and it went more smoothly now. Parry knew they were on another road. He got his head halfway out of the blanket.

He said, "You told them to go ahead and look."

"I had to," she said. "I knew they would look anyway. I had to take the chance."

"Do you think we'll be stopped again?"

"No. From here on it's going to be all right."

"Everything's going to be all right," Parry said. He looked at the back of his hand. His teeth had gone in deep. The blood wouldn't stop. And his elbows were beginning to hurt again. And he wanted a drink of water. He wanted a cigarette. He wanted to go to sleep.

He closed his eyes and tried to get comfortable. Maybe he could fall asleep.

She said, "How's it going?"

"Dandy. Everything's going to be all right and everything's dandy."

"Stop it, Vincent. You're free."

"Free as the breeze. I don't have a worry in the world. I'm doing great and everything's dandy. Look, if you're not the police, who are you?"

"I'm your friend. Is that enough?"

"No," Parry said. "It's not enough. If they catch me they catch me, but in the meantime I want to stay out as long as I can. And I won't stay out long if I make mistakes. I want to be sure this isn't a mistake. How did you know I was on that road?"

"I didn't. That is, I wasn't sure. But I had a feeling—"

"You had a feeling. So you went to a fortune and he told you Vincent Parry broke out of San Quentin and was going into the hills and through the woods and getting a lift in a Studebaker."

"Don't make fun of fortune tellers." Her voice was light. He wondered if she was smiling.

He raised his head a few more inches from the blanket. He could see her blonde hair above the grey velour upholstery. All he had to do was get hold of her hair and pull her head back to get a crack at her jaw.

"How did you know I broke out of San Quentin?" he asked.

"The radio."

He brought his head up another inch. He said, "All right, that passes. Let's try this one—how did you know I was on that road?"

"I know the section."

"What are you giving me?"

"I'm telling you I know the section." Her voice was no longer light. "I know all the roads around here. The first radio announcement said you got away. The second announcement said you got away in a truck. They gave the location where police stopped the truck. I know the section very well. I used to paint."

"You used to paint what?"

"Water color. Landscape stuff. I used to hang around there and paint those meadows and hills. Sometimes I'd go into the hills and I'd get a slant on the woods. Then

32

sometimes I'd use the road to get another slant on the woods. That's how I knew about the road. I had a feeling you'd be on that road."

"I'm supposed to believe that."

"Don't you want to believe it? Then don't believe it. Do you want to get out?"

"What?"

"I said do you want to get out? I got you past the police. If you had taken that Studebaker you'd be on your way back to San Quentin by now. That's one thing. And if they had pulled back that blanket another few inches I'd be letting myself in for a few years of prison. That's another thing. Right now I'm letting myself in for a broken jaw."

"What do you mean a broken jaw?"

"You're all set to clip me one, aren't you?"

Parry said, "Now I know why you stick up for the fortune tellers. You're a fortune teller yourself. You're a mind reader."

"Please, Vincent. Please wait it out."

"Wait for what?"

"For the chance. A real chance. There's going to be a real chance for you. I have the feeling— —"

"Let's try a hard one," Parry said. "Tell me the date of my birth."

"April first, the way you're acting now. Do you want to get out?"

"You want to get rid of me, don't you?"

"Yes."

"Why?"

"I'm beginning to feel afraid."

"Sister, I don't blame you. The law— —"

"I'm not afraid of the law, Vincent. I'm afraid of you. I'm sorry I started this. I'm sorry I threw the blanket in the back of the car and went out to find you. Now I've found you and I'm stuck with you. I didn't know it would be this way."

33

"What way?"

"You. The way you're carrying on. I thought it would be very different from what it is. I thought you'd be soft. And kind. And very grateful. Very grateful for every little thing. That's the way I always imagined you. That's the way you were at the trial."

"You attended the trial?"

"Yes. I was there almost every day."

"How come?"

"I was interested."

"In me?"

"Yes."

"Sorry for me?"

"Yes. At the trial. And after you were sentenced. And earlier today. Now I'm no longer interested. I did something I wanted to do very badly. I did my little bit for you. And it hasn't turned out the way I thought it would turn out. You're not soft, Vincent. You're mean — and I'm stuck with you."

"You're not stuck with me," Parry said. "I'm getting out here. And I'm not doing what I did to Studebaker. All I'm doing is saying good-bye and good luck."

The Pontiac went over to the side of the road and came to a stop.

"How is it?" Parry said.

"It's clear."

"Any place I can duck?"

"Take a look."

He brought his head up and gazed through all the windows. Directly ahead the wide road sliced through a narrow valley devoid of houses. On the right side the valley widened and on the left side there was a patch of woodland going level for a few hundred yards and then climbing up a mountain.

"This will be all right," Parry said. He put his hand on the door handle. He tilted the back of the empty front

34

seat, quickly opened the door and leaped out. Running toward the patch of woodland he heard the Pontiac going away.

He was twenty yards away from the woodland when he heard a motor grinding and without looking he knew that the Pontiac was in reverse and coming back. He turned and raced toward the road.

The door was open for him.

She said, "Get in."

He jumped in, closed the door and got under the blanket as if it were home and he had been away from home for a long time.

The Pontiac started forward and went into second and moved up to third and did forty. She held it there.

Parry said, "Why did you come back?"

"You looked lonely out there."

"I felt lonely."

"How do you feel now?"

"Better."

"Much better?"

"Much."

For a while they didn't say anything. Then Parry asked her if it was all right to smoke and she opened both side windows and tossed a book of matches over her shoulder. She asked him to light one for her. He lit two cigarettes, reached up and gave her one, then got down under the blanket and pulled smoke into his mouth. The smoke aggravated the heat that was already in the blanket. He didn't mind. He found that the thirst was going away and going along with it was the pain in his elbows and the back of his hand had stopped bleeding.

She said, "I forgot something."

"You mean you left something with the police?"

"No, I forgot something when I said you weren't soft, the way I'd expected you'd be. When I said you were mean. I forgot that you were in a prison for seven months. Of

35

course you're mean. Anyone would be mean. But don't be mean to me. Promise me you won't be mean to me."

"Look, I told you before—you're not stuck with me."

"But I am, Vincent. I am."

Parry took the cigarette from his mouth, put it in again and took a long tug. He got the smoke out and then he sighed. He said, "It's too much for me."

She didn't answer that. Parry felt the car turning, going slower, heard the sound of San Francisco coming in and getting under the blanket. The sound of other automobiles and the honking of horns, the hum of trade and the droning of people on the streets. He was frightened again. He wanted to get away from here and fast. He began remembering pictures he had seen in travel folders long ago. Places that looked out upon water. Lovely beaches. One was Patavilca, Peru. Another was Almeria, Spain. There were so many others, it was such a big world.

The Pontiac came to a stop.

CHAPTER 4

Parry got his head past the edge of the blanket. He said, "What's the matter?"

"We're at my place. It's an apartment house. We're on Geary, not far from the center of town. Are you ready?"

"Ready for what?"

"You're going to get out of the car. You're going to stay at my place."

"That's no good."

"Can you think of anything better?"

Parry tried to think of something better. He thought of the railroad station and he threw it away. He thought of hopping a freight and he knew they'd be watching the freight yards. They'd be watching every channel of possible getaway.

He said, "No."

"Then get ready, Vincent. Count up to fifteen. By that time I'll be in the apartment house and the elevator will be set to go up. When you reach fifteen get out of the car and walk fast but don't run. And don't be scared."

"What's there to be scared about?"

"Come on, Vincent. Don't be scared. It's all right now.

We've reached home."

"There's no place like home," Parry said.

"Start counting, Vincent," she said and then she was out of the car and the door closed again and Parry was counting. When he reached fifteen he told himself that he couldn't do it. He was shaking again. This wasn't her apartment house. This was her way of getting rid of him. What did she need him for? What good could he do her? She had the keys to the car and now she was taking a stroll. When he got out of the car he would see there was no apartment house and no open door and nothing. He told himself that he couldn't get out of the car and he couldn't remain in the car.

He got out of the car and faced a six-story yellow brick apartment house. The front door was half-way open. He closed the door of the Pontiac. Then he walked quickly across the pavement, up the steps of the apartment house.

Then they were in the elevator and it was going up. It stopped at the third floor. The corridor was done in dark yellow. The door of her apartment was green. The number on the door was 307. She opened the door and went in and he followed.

It was a small apartment. It was expensive. The general idea was grey-violet, with yellow here and there. Parry reached for a ball of yellow glass that had a lighter attachment on top. He lighted a cigarette and tossed the empty pack into a grey-violet wastebasket. He looked at a yellow-stained radio with a phonograph annex. Then he found himself glancing at the record albums grouped in a yellow case beside the yellow-stained cabinet.

"I see you go in for swing," he said.

From another room she said, "Legitimate swing."

He heard a door closing and knew she was in the bathroom. All he had to do now was open the door that faced the corridor. Then down the corridor and out by way of the fire escape. And then where?

Dragging on the cigarette he stooped over and began going through the record albums. When he came to Basie he frowned. There was a lot of Basie. The best Basie. The same Basie he liked. There was *Every Tub* and *Swinging the Blues* and *Texas Shuffle*. There was *John's Idea* and *Lester Leaps In* and *Out the Window*. He took a glance at the window. He came back to the records and decided to play *Texas Shuffle*. He remembered that every time he played *Texas Shuffle* he got a picture of countless steers parading fast across an endless plain in Texas. He switched on the current and got the record under the needle. *Texas Shuffle* began to roll softly and it was very lovely. It clicked with the fact that he had a cigarette in his mouth, watching the smoke go up, and the police didn't know he was here.

Texas Shuffle was hitting its climax when she came out of the bathroom. Parry turned and looked at her. She smiled at him.

She said, "You like Basie?"

"I collect him. That is, I did."

"What else do you like?"

"Gin."

"Straight?"

"Yes. With a drink of water after every three or four."

She stopped smiling. She said, "There's something odd about that."

"Odd about what?"

"I also go for gin. The same way. The same chaser schedule."

He said nothing. She went into another room. The record ended and Parry got Basie started with *John's Idea*. The idea was well under way and Basie's right hand was doing wonderful things on the keys and then she was coming in with a tray that had two glasses and two jiggers, a bottle of gin and a pitcher of water.

She poured the gin. Parry watched her while he listened

to the jumping music. She gave him some gin and he threw it down his throat while she was filling her jigger. He helped himself to a second jigger. He lit another cigarette. She put on another record, and sat down in a violet chair, leaning back and gazing at the ceiling.

"Light me a cigarette," she said.

He usually smoked a bit wet but he lighted her cigarette dry. As she took it from him she leaned over to lift the needle from the finished record.

"More?" she said.

"No. Let's talk instead. Let's talk about what's going to be."

"Do you have plans already?"

"No."

"I do, Vincent. I think you should live here for a while. Live here until the excitement dies down and an opening presents itself."

Parry picked himself up from the floor. He walked to the window and looked out. The street was almost empty. He saw smoke coming from a row of stacks beyond rooftops. He took himself away from the window and looked at a grey-violet wall.

He said, "If I had a lot of money I could understand it. The way it is now I don't get it at all. There's nothing in this for you. Nothing but aggravation and hardship."

He heard her getting up from the chair, walking out of the room. From another room he heard a sound of a bureau drawer getting opened. Then she was coming back and saying, "I want to show you something."

He turned and she handed him a clipping. He recognized the print. It was from the *Chronicle*. It was a letter to the editor.

There's a great deal to be said in behalf of Vincent

40

Parry, the man now on trial for the murder of his wife. I don't expect you to print this letter, because the issue will be ultimately settled in court and from the looks of things it is a fair trial and Parry has his own lawyer. And yet the prosecution has steadily aimed at getting away from the technical aspects of the case and attempted to picture Parry as a combination of unfaithful husband, killer and draft dodger. I am not acquainted with Parry's marital difficulties. As for the killer angle, the case is not yet completed and further testimony will no doubt bring up new facts that will decide the matter one way or another. However, I am certain that Vincent Parry is not a draft dodger. I happen to know that Parry made several attempts to enter the armed forces even though he had been rejected previously because of physical disability.

The letter was signed — Irene Janney.

Parry said, "Is that you?"

"Yes."

"It's not much of a letter. It hardly says anything."

"It's not the entire letter. The *Chronicle* couldn't print all of it. They'd have to use a couple of columns. But they tried to be fair. They included that contradiction of the draft-dodging angle."

"How did you know I tried to get in?"

She pressed her cigarette in a yellow glass ash tray. "I have a friend who works at your draft board. He told me. He said you were called up twice and rejected. He said you kept pestering the draft board for another chance to get in."

"Is that what got you interested in the case?"

"No," Irene said. "This friend knew I was interested. He called me up and told me what had happened at the draft board. He told me you really wanted to get in. It checked

41

with the way I felt about the entire affair. Sometimes I get that way. I get excited about something and I give it everything I have."

"I think I'll clear out," Parry said.

"Sit down. Let's keep talking. Let's tell each other about ourselves. How's the kidney trouble?"

"I've been feeling better," Parry said. He lit another cigarette.

"It's odd about the kidney trouble."

"Why?"

"I have it also. Not serious, but it bothers me now and then."

"Look, I think I'll clear out. How's the fire escape?"

"Stay here, Vincent."

"What for?"

"Stay until it's dark at least."

He looked at the stained-yellow cabinet, the unmoving shining black record on the phonograph disc. He said, "It's this way. I've got to keep moving. And moving fast. Like this it's no good. The police will be working while I'm doing nothing. They're running after me and if I don't run I'll be caught."

"There's a time to run."

He was about to say something but just then the phone rang. It was a French phone, yellow. It was on a yellow table beside the grey-violet davenport. Irene picked up the phone.

"Hello—oh, hello Bob. How are you—yes, I'm fine—tonight? Oh, I'm sorry, Bob, but I won't be able to make it tonight—no, no other commitments, but I just don't feel like going out.—Oh yes, I'm quite all right, but I'm in the mood for a quiet evening and reading and the radio and so forth all by myself—no, I just feel that way—don't be silly—oh, don't be silly Bob—well, maybe tomorrow—oh, Bob don't be silly—stop it, Bob, I don't like to hear you talk that way. Call me tomorrow—yes, tomorrow about

seven. —Of course not. How's your work coming along—
that's fine—all right, Bob—yes, tomorrow at seven I'll
expect to hear from you. Good-by—"

Parry walked toward the door.

She stood up and stepped between Parry and the door.
She said, "Please, Vincent—"

"I'm going," he said. "That phone call did it."

"But I didn't want to see him anyway."

"All right, but there will be times when you'll want to
see him. And times when you want to be at certain places.
Doing certain things. And you won't be able to, because
you'll be stuck with me."

"But I said only for tonight."

"Tonight will be a beginning. And if we let it begin it
will keep on going. You're trying to help me but you won't
be helping me. And I certainly won't be helping you any.
We'll only get in each other's way. I'm going."

"Just until tonight, Vincent. Until it gets dark."

"Dark. They won't see me when it's dark." He stood
there staring at the door as she stepped away from him and
went into another room. He didn't know what she was
doing in the other room. When she came back she had a
tape measure in her hand. He looked at the tape measure
and then he looked at her face.

She said, "I'm going to buy you some clothes."

"When?"

"Right now. I want the exact measurements. I want the
fit to be perfect. And it's got to be expensive clothes. I
know a place near here—"

She took his measurements. He didn't say anything. She
took the measurements and then she made notes in a small
memo book. He watched her going into another room.
Again he heard the sound of a bureau drawer getting
opened. As she came out again she was counting a roll of
bills. A thick roll.

"No," Parry said. "Let's forget about it. I'm going

43

now—"

"You're staying," she said. "I'm going. And I'll be back soon. While you wait here you can be doing things. Like getting rid of those rags you're wearing. All of them, even the shoes. Take them into the kitchen. You'll find wrapping paper there. Make a bundle and throw it into the incinerator. Then go into the bathroom and treat yourself to a hot shower. Nice and hot and plenty of soap. And you need a shave." A little laugh got out before she could stop it.

"What's the laugh for?"

"I was thinking you could use his razor. It's a Swedish hollow-ground safety razor. I used to be married and I gave it to my husband for a Christmas present. He didn't like it. I used it every now and then when I went to the beach. I stopped using it when someone told me depilatory cream was better."

"What happened to your husband?"

"He took a walk."

"When was this?"

"Long, long ago. I was twenty-three when we married and it lasted sixteen months and two weeks and three days. He told me I was too easy to get along with and it was getting dull. I just remembered there's no shaving soap. But I've got some skin cream. You can rub that in and then use the ordinary soap and you won't cut yourself. The incinerator is next to the sink. Don't forget to get every stitch of those clothes into the bundle. Maybe you better make two bundles so you'll be sure they get down."

"All right, I'll make two bundles."

She was at the door now. She said, "I'll be back soon. Is there anything special you want?"

"No."

"Will you do me a favor, Vincent?"

"What?"

"Will you be here when I come back?"

"Maybe."

"I want to know, Vincent."

"All right, I'll be here."

"What colors do you like?"

"Grey," he said. "Grey and violet." He wanted to laugh. He didn't laugh. "Sometimes a bit of yellow here and there."

She opened the door and left the apartment. Parry stood a few feet away from the door and looked at the door for several minutes. Then he walked back to the tray where the gin was and he poured himself two shots and got them down fast. He took a drink of water, went into the kitchen and found the wrapping paper. He undressed, slowly at first, then gradually faster as he realized he was getting rid of Studebaker's clothes and they were dirty clothes. For the first time he was aware that they had a smell and they were itchy. It was a pleasure to take them off and throw them away. Now he was naked and he was making two bundles. He got a ball of string from the kitchen cabinet, tied the bundles securely, then let them go down the incinerator. He heard the swishing noise as the bundles dropped, the vague thud that told him they had reached bottom. Knowing that Studebaker's clothes and the prison shoes were going to burn and become ashes he felt slightly happy.

He walked into the bathroom. It was yellow tile, all of it. There was a glassed-in shower and he got it started and used a rectangle of lavender soap. He made the shower very hot, then soaped himself well, got the hot water on again, switched to full cold, let it hit him for the better part of a minute. Then he was out of the shower, using a thick yellow towel that he could have used as a cape.

The skin cream mixed well with the soap, resulting in a decent lather that gave the razor a smooth ride. He shaved in three minutes and then he went into the parlor and lit a cigarette. He had the yellow towel wrapped around his middle and tucked in. He looked over the Basie records and decided to play *Shorty George*.

He let the needle go down and just as it touched the black he felt something coming into the apartment. It was only a noise but to him it had form and the ability to clutch and rip at his insides.

It was the buzzer.

Parry lifted the needle and stopped the phonograph. He waited.

The buzzer sounded again. Parry slowly lifted the cigarette to his lips and took a long haul. He sat down on the edge of the davenport and waited. He gazed at the phone attachment beside the door and as the buzzer hit him again he decided to lift the phone and tell the person down there to go away and leave him alone. He let his head go into cupped hands.

Then the buzzing stopped.

The tears started again, coming into his eyes, collecting there, ready to gush. He told himself that he had to stop that sort of thing. It was bad because it was soft and if there was anything he couldn't afford now it was softness. The lukewarm and weak brand of softness. Everything had to be ice, and just as hard, and just as fast as a whippet and just as smooth. And just as accurate as a calculating machine, giving the buzzer a certain denomination. Now that the buzzer had stopped a key was clicking into position and crossing off the denomination. The buzzer had stopped and it was all over. The person down there had gone away. Check that off. Then check off all the other things that needed checking off. Get another key in position and check off San Quentin. Go back further than that and check off the trial. Come back to San Quentin, go ahead of San Quentin and check off the barrel and the truck, the pale-green meadow, the hills and the dark-green woods. Check off the Studebaker, the man in the Studebaker, the ride to San Francisco and the motorcycle cops.

Check off Studebaker's clothes. Get started with now and keep going from now. Check off the buzzer. Start *Shorty George* again.

He turned the lever that started the phonograph running.

The black record began to spin. He put the needle down and *Shorty George* was on its way. Parry stood a few feet away from the phonograph, watching the record go round and listening to the Basie band riding into the fourth dimension. He recognized the Buck Clayton trumpet and he smiled. The smile was wet clay and it became cement when he heard knuckles rapping against the apartment door.

All of him was cement.

The rapping was in series, going against *Shorty George*. The first series stopped and Parry tried to get to the phonograph so he could cut off the music that wasn't music anymore, only a lot of noise telling the person out there that someone was in the apartment. He couldn't get to the phonograph because he couldn't budge. The second series of raps came to him, stopped for a few moments and then the third series was on and he counted three insistent raps.

Then he knew it was impossible to check off all those things. They were things to be remembered and considered. This thing now rapping at the door was the police. It was logical that they should be here. It wasn't logical for them to have slipped up on that blanket episode. Then again it was logical for them to have taken the Pontiac's license number as the car went away from them. It was easy to sketch—them talking it over, telling each other they should have looked further under the blanket to see what was in those old clothes for China, then congratulating each other on their brains in taking the license number, and now coming here to have a talk with Irene Janney.

He turned and looked around the room and tried to see

47

something. The window was the only thing he saw. *Shorty George* was rounding the far turn and coming toward the homestretch, but he didn't hear it, he was staring at the window.

The fourth series of raps got through the door and bounced around the room, and following the raps a voice said, "Irene—are you there?"

It belonged to a woman. Then it couldn't be the police. And yet there was something about the voice that was worse than the police.

"Irene—open the door."

The music was music again. Parry figured if he made the music louder he wouldn't hear the voice.

It was a voice he knew and he was trying to place it and he didn't want to place it. He made the music louder.

"Irene—what's the matter? Let me in."

Shorty George was coming down the homestretch. The voice outside the door was louder than *Shorty George.*

"Irene—I know you're in there and I want you to let me in."

The voice was getting him now, closing in on him, forceps of sound that was more than sound, because now he recognized the voice, the pestering voice that belonged to Madge Rapf.

CHAPTER 5

It was as if the door was glass and he could see her standing out there, the Pest. His eyes made a turn and looked at the ball of yellow glass with the lighter attachment. All he had to do was grab hold of that thing and open the door, go out there and start banging her over the head to shut her up. This wouldn't be the first time he had liked the idea of banging her over the head.

"Irene—I don't think this is a bit funny and I want you to open the door."

Parry reached over and picked up the heavy ball of yellow glass.

"Irene—are you going to open the door?"

Parry tested the weight of the ball of yellow glass.

"Irene—you know I'm out here. What's the matter with you?"

Parry took a step toward the door. He wasn't shaking and he wondered why. He wasn't perspiring and he wasn't shaking and the ball of yellow glass was steady and all set in his right hand. He wondered why he felt so glad about this and all at once he understood he was about to do mankind a favor.

"Irene—do you intend to open the door?"

Shorty George crossed the finish line and the glazed center spun soundlessly under the needle.

Rapping again. Angry, puzzled rapping.

"Irene—open the door."

Parry took another step toward the door and he began to shake. He began to perspire. His teeth were vibrating. A grinding noise started deep in his belly and worked its way up toward his mouth.

"Irene—"

"Shut up," Parry yelled, realized that he was yelling, tried to hold it, couldn't do anything about it. "For God's sake—shut up."

"What?"

"I said shut up. Go away."

He knew that she was stepping back and away from the door, looking at the number to see if she had the right apartment.

Then she said something that was Madge Rapf all over. She said, "Irene, is someone in there with you?"

"Yes, someone's in here with her," Parry said. "Now go away."

"Oh, I didn't know."

"Well, now you know. So go away."

She went away. Parry had an ear next to the door crack and he could hear her footsteps going down the corridor toward the elevator. He moved to the phonograph and picked up the needle from the silent record. He lit another cigarette and then took a position near the window and waited there. He estimated two minutes and it was slightly under two minutes when he saw Madge Rapf getting past the partition of yellow brick. He knew she was going to turn and have a look at the window and he ducked just as she turned. When he came up she was on her way again and he watched her crossing the street. He figured she had

50

to cross the street but when she got to the other side he knew that was wrong. She was there because she wanted to get a better view of the window.

He kept one eye past the limit of the window. He didn't know whether she could see that half of his face. But even if she could see that one half of face she wouldn't be able to recognize it. Now she came walking down the other side of the street and stopped when she was directly across from the apartment house. She stood there and looked at the window. Her head went low and that meant she was looking at the grey Pontiac. Then the window again. Then the Pontiac. Then the window. Then she started on down the street. Then she stopped and took another look at the window. She took a few steps in the direction of the apartment house. She hesitated, then came on.

"For God's sake—" Parry murmured.

She stopped again. This time she made a definite about-face and walked on and kept on walking.

Parry looked at the door and he was about to make a go for it when he remembered that his attire consisted of a yellow towel and nothing more. He sucked at the cigarette and walked without meaning in a small circle and then he went back to the window. No Madge Rapf. But something else. This time it was a policeman on the other side of the street. The policeman didn't look at the apartment house. Parry crossed to the davenport and sat on the edge, the cigarette burning furiously as he gave it the works.

Something pulled him up from the davenport and he went into the kitchen. It was small and white and spotless. He put his hand on a solid bar of glass, the handle of the refrigerator. He opened the door and looked at the food without knowing why he was looking at it. He looked at a neat row of oranges and then he closed the door. He looked at the kitchen cabinet, the sink, the floor—the incinerator. He opened the metal cap of the incinerator and gazed into the black hole. He closed the incinerator, went out of the kitchen and into the bathroom. When he came out of the bathroom he went into the one room that was left, the bedroom.

The bedroom was all yellow. Pale yellow broadloom rug and furniture and dark yellow walls. Four water-color landscapes that weren't bad. They were signed "Irene Janney." He recognized the pale-green meadow and the hills. And again he saw the dark-green woods and the road. He wanted another cigarette and he went into the parlor.

When he came back to the bedroom he stood in front of the bureau and ran his fingers cross the shining yellow wood. He puffed hard at the cigarette and then he opened the top drawer. It was divided into two sections. There was a big bottle of violet cologne that would follow the half-filled bottle on top of the bureau. There was a carton of Luckies, two jars of skin cream, a pile of handkerchiefs wrapped in a sachet-scented fold of grey-violet satin. There was a box filled with various sorts of buttons. That was about all for the top drawer.

The second drawer had underthings and more handkerchiefs and three handbags. They were expensive. Everything was expensive. Everything was neat and clean. The third drawer was about the same. The fourth drawer was heaped with papers and note-books and text-books. Parry examined the papers and books. He found out that Irene Janney had attended the University of Oregon, had majored in sociology, had graduated in 1939. There were considerable examination papers and theses and most of them were marked B. There was a record book from the Class of '39 and he followed the alphabetical order until he came to her picture and write-up. Her picture was nothing special. She was even thinner then than now, and she was plenty thin now. She looked uncertain and worried, as if she was afraid of what would happen to her after graduation.

There was something at the bottom of the drawer peeping out from the edge of a textbook. It was from a newspaper. It became a clipping as Parry took it out. He saw the picture of a man who looked something like Irene. The picture was captioned "Dies in Prison." Underneath the picture was the name Calvin Janney. Alongside the picture was an article headed "Road Ends for Janney."

Calvin Janney, sentenced four years ago to life imprisonment for the murder of his wife, died last night in San Quentin prison. He had been ill for the past several months. Officials said Janney made a death-bed statement claiming his innocence, the same claim he made during the sensational trial in San Francisco.

Janney, a wealthy real-estate broker, was accused of killing his bride of a second marriage, less than a week after they had celebrated their first wedding anniversary. Death was attributed to a skull fracture caused by a heavy blow with an ornamental brass jar. The body had been found at the foot of a staircase in the Janney home. Janney stated that his wife had fallen down the stairs, had knocked the brass jar from the base of the banister in her descent, then had struck her head on the jar. This statement was disproved by the prosecution. It was established that Janney had charged his wife with infidelity and had threatened on several occasions to kill her. Janney's fingerprints on the brass jar was a primary factor in the guilty verdict.

Efforts to obtain a new trial proved fruitless. In recent months Janney's attorneys made another plea founded on new developments, the result of continued investigation during the past four years. The plea made no headway due to lack of witnesses.

Janney was 54. He is survived by a son, Burton, a chemical engineer in Portland. Also a daughter, Irene, a grade-school student in the same city.

There was a date at the top of the clipping. It said February 9, 1928. Parry kept looking at the date. On the basis of the date and the record-book date, she was nine when her father died and she was five when the trial took place. He read the clipping again. Then again. He decided she ought to be coming back soon and maybe he ought to get the clipping and the papers and books back in the drawer. He started to handle the clipping and he was getting it back in the textbook when he heard the door opening into the parlor and footsteps coming into the apartment, going through the parlor, coming into the bedroom.

She looked at him. She looked at the clipping half in his hand and half in the textbook. Her arms were filled with paper boxes and she put these on the bed and kept on looking at Parry, looking at the clipping, then back to Parry.

"Did you get rid of the clothes?" she said.

"Yes. I made two bundles and threw them down the incinerator."

"How was the razor?"

"Fine."

"That shower and shave did you a world of good. How do you feel?"

"Fine," Parry said.

She pointed to the open drawer. "What's the big idea?"

"I didn't have anything to do."

"All right, let's close the drawer, shall we?"

Parry got the clipping into the textbook, got the text-book back in the drawer along with the other books and papers. He closed the drawer.

She pointed to the closed drawer. "Anything happen while I was away—outside of that?"

"You had a caller." He wondered why he was telling her.

Irene frowned. "I hope you didn't answer the buzzer."

"No, I didn't answer the buzzer. But she came up and she knocked on the door."

"A she?"

"Yes. She talked to you through the door. I stayed there and let her talk. It would have been all right except I had the phonograph going and she could hear it. She kept asking you to open the door. Finally I told her to go away."

The frown went deeper. "That wasn't such a bright idea."

"I know. It got out before I could stop it."

"Did she argue with you?"

"No. She went away. Does that close it?"

"I hope so."

"What do you mean you hope so?" Parry asked.

"Well, my friends know I don't go in for that sort of thing. Now they'll think—"

"All right, let me get into those clothes and scram out of here."

"Wait," Irene said. "I didn't mean that. I don't care what they think. I'm only trying to be technical. And very careful."

"Let's see the clothes."

She sat down on the edge of the bed and looked at him. Then she blinked a few times and lowered her head. She put a forefinger to the space between her eyes and pressed there and took it around in little circles.

Parry leaned back against the bureau. He said, "You're tired, aren't you?"

"Headache."

"Got any aspirins?"

55

"In the bathroom cabinet."

He went into the bathroom, came back with two aspirins and a glass half-filled with water. She smiled at him. She took the aspirins and drank all the water. He took the glass back to the bathroom. When he came back to the bedroom she was opening the paper boxes.

It amounted to almost a wardrobe. Four shirts, three white and one grey. Five neckties, three grey and two on a grey-violet theme. Five sets of underwear and a stack of handkerchiefs. Six pairs of grey socks. A grey worsted suit with a vertical suggestion of violet. A pair of tan straight-tipped blucher shoes. And grey suspenders.

There were other things. A military brush and a comb. A toothbrush and a jar of shaving cream and a safety razor.

She arranged the things neatly on the bed and then she went out of the room. Parry got started with the clothes. Everything fitted perfectly. His hair was still damp from the shower and it moved nicely under the brush and comb. He had on one of the white shirts and a grey-violet tie and he put a white handkerchief in the breast pocket of the grey worsted suit. He felt very new and shining.

He walked into the parlor.

Irene was sitting on the davenport and when she saw him she smiled and said, "Well — hello."

"Okay?"

"Very okay."

"I bet you paid plenty."

"I like to spend money for clothes."

"What did you tell them?"

"I said I had a boy friend just discharged from the Army and I wanted to surprise him with a complete new outfit. They're a small, exclusive store and they don't like to be hurried. But it was a big order and they didn't want to lose it, and anyway there wasn't much work to be done

56

on the suit."

"How's the headache?"

"Better."

"That's good. Thanks for the clothes."

"You're welcome, Vincent. You're really very welcome. And I've got something else for you." She opened a handbag, took the wrapping from a flat white case. She handed it to him.

It contained a round waterproof-type wrist watch, chromium plated with a grey suede strap.

Parry looked at the wrist watch. He said, "Why this?"

"You'll need a watch. That's one of the things you'll really need."

He put the watch on his wrist. He said, "You're laying out a lot of money. Can you afford it?"

"What do you think?"

"I've got an idea you can afford it."

"You've got the right idea," she said. "Now tell me where you got it."

"From the clipping."

Her eyes were soft. Her lips weren't curved but it was a smile anyway. She said, "Vincent, will you always be that way with me?"

"What way?"

"Honest."

"Yes. I'll be that way with you until we say good-by. It's getting dark now. It's almost time to say good-by."

She stood up. She said, "Let's have dinner. I'm not a bad cook. Do you like fried chicken?"

"Better than anything."

"Same here," she said, and then they were looking at each other. She started a smile, started to lose it, got it again when he smiled at her. They stood there smiling at each other. He reached toward the cigarette box and she said, "Light one for me," and then she went into the kitchen.

He lit two cigarettes, went into the kitchen, saw her putting on an apron. She was tying the apron strings. She gestured with her lips and he put the cigarette in her mouth and walked out of the kitchen.

"Let's have some music," she said.

"Radio?"

"Yes, put the radio on."

He got the radio working. A small studio orchestra was trying to do something with *Holiday for Strings* but there weren't enough strings. Toward the middle most of the orchestra seemed to be taking a holiday. Parry went over to a circular mirror at the other side of the room and looked at himself and admired the grey suit. He fingered the necktie and then he touched the smoothness of the suede wrist-watch strap. Looking at the wrist watch he told himself it was fast. It couldn't be eight already. He turned toward the window. The San Francisco sky was greying.

Irene came in and said dinner was ready. She really knew how to fry a chicken. She opened a bottle of Sauterne and he knew before he took the first taste it was high-priced wine. He told her she was a good cook. She smiled and didn't say anything. For dessert they had butterscotch pudding. She told him she had a weakness for butterscotch pudding and made it three times a week. He asked her if she ate out much and she said no, she liked her own cooking and besides restaurants these days were an ordeal.

They had black coffee and then they sat there smoking cigarettes. He offered to help her with the dishes and she said no, she could do them in a jiffy. He went into the parlor and she did the dishes in a jiffy. Parry took another look at the sky and it was getting dark. He was watching it get darker as Irene came into the parlor. She followed his gaze out the window. She followed his gaze to the wrist watch.

She said, "Don't go. Stay here tonight. You can sleep on the davenport."

"That's out. We've got maybe thirty minutes and then I'm on my way. And now I want to ask you something. Where is your brother?"

"Dead. He was in a terrible automobile accident six years ago. What you really want to know is how I got my money. And that's how. My father willed it to Burton, and then in the hospital, just before he died, Burton willed it to me. It amounts to a couple hundred thousand dollars."

"That's a lot of cash."

"It's good to have. It's the only thing I have."

"What about your husband?"

"I received the final decree a few months ago. I don't know where he is. Do you want the name?"

"Why should I want the name?"

"Why should you want to know where I got my money?"

"Curious. You didn't get it with water colors. I knew that. And you didn't get it through sociology. I knew that. So I went back to the clipping and I wanted to check on it and I wanted to know why you had it and not your brother. Was this where you lived with your husband?"

"No."

"What kind of guy was your husband?"

"A louse."

"When did you find it out?"

"The first week."

"Why didn't you leave?"

She said, "I had the money and I had me and I had him. I wasn't much interested in the money. That left me and him. He liked to drink, but that was all right, so did I. And he liked to gamble and that wasn't so good, because he had an idea he knew poker and he didn't know the first thing about poker. Even nights when we stayed home together he wanted to play poker and one night I took him for every cent he made that month. I think that was the only thing he liked about me—the fact that I could make him look sick when it came to poker."

"What was his line?"

"All right, Vincent, I'll tell you about him. His name is George Hagedorn and I met him three years ago. We knew each other four months and then we got married. We were a couple of lonely people and I guess that was the only reason we married. He didn't know I had money. I told him a few days after the wedding and it didn't seem to make much difference. I guess that was one of the very few things that was good about him. He had a lot of pride. Maybe too much. I think that was why he gambled. I think that was the only way he reasoned he could get money with his own hands. He hadn't tried many other ways because he was very lazy. One of the laziest men I've ever seen. When we married he was thirty-two and a complete failure. A statistician making forty-five a week in an investment security house."

"What house?"

"Kinney."

"I know that firm," Parry said. "They're big. Offices in Santa Barbara and Philly. I can't figure Santa Barbara."

"He tried to get transferred down to Santa Barbara but they didn't need him there. He wouldn't have lasted at the office here but he had asthma and it kept him out of the Army and I guess they figured they might as well keep him for the duration. Besides, they had him broken in. But he was late and absent a lot and I guess they finally got fed up with him. About a year ago I tried to get in touch with him and I called Kinney and they said he didn't work there any more. They didn't know where he was."

"Why did you want to get in touch with him?"

"I was lonely. I wanted a date."

"What about Bob?"

"I had an idea you'd remember that. You remember things, don't you."

"Certain things stick in my mind. What about Bob?"

"That was during a time when I wasn't seeing Bob. Every now and then it happens that way."

"What way?"

"Well, I get afraid. Or maybe it's my conscience, because he's married. Not really married. He's separated, but his wife won't give him a divorce. She doesn't want him and at the same time she won't let anyone else have him. She gets a kick out of it. But I don't have to tell you, Vincent. You know what she is. You know who she is."

CHAPTER 6

Parry looked at the window. Now it was dark grey out there and getting darker. He said, "I better be going."

"She worked against you at the trial, Vincent. She works against everybody. She has a way about her. She won't leave people alone. And the way she pesters me—"

"The way she pesters you has nothing to do with me," Parry said. He got up and moved toward the door. "All I know is she couldn't see me through the door and she didn't see me through the window. That's all I want to know. You've been good to me. I won't forget it but I want you to forget it. Being good to people sounds nice but it's hard work. From here on there's only one person you'll need to be good to. That's yourself. Good-by, Irene."

"Good-by, Vincent. Wait, you've got things here. I'll put them in a grip—"

He opened the door and walked out. He looked up and down the corridor and then he stepped quickly to the elevator. When he reached the street he saw it was even darker than it had looked from the window. He walked quickly, walked south, searching for a drugstore. Three blocks and then he saw a drugstore and instinctively his hand went into the right side-pocket of the grey worsted trousers, groping for change. His fingers touched paper and he was taking bills from the pocket. All new bills, crisp and bright. It amounted to a thousand dollars. Eight one-hundred dollar bills. Two fifties. The rest in tens and fives. He wondered how she knew he kept his money in the right side-pocket of his trousers. He started toward the drugstore, then told himself a telephone call was out. A taxi made a turn and started slowly up the street. Parry stepped to the curb and raised his arm.

The taxi came to a reluctant stop. The driver was a thick-faced man close to forty. The driver said, "How far? I'm on my way to a fare."

"It's not far."

The driver examined the grey worsted suit. "North?"

"Yes. A couple miles. Just keep going north and I'll tell you how to get there."

"All right, hop in. Mind a little speed?"

"I like speed."

The taxi went into a sprint, made a lot of wracking noise as it turned a corner to get on a wider street. Parry sat low, trying to get his face away from the rear-view mirror because he sensed the driver was studying the mirror. He wondered why the driver was studying the mirror.

"That's a nice suit you're wearing," the driver said.

"I'm glad you like it. What are we doing?"

"Forty. Another turn and we'll do fifty. On this kind of deal I usually take her up to sixty."

"What do you mean this kind of a deal?" He could see the driver grinning at him in the rear-view mirror. He wondered why the driver was grinning.

"A double job," the driver said. "Two fares on one trip. Is your trip really necessary?"

"Sort of," Parry said.

"It's crazy the way they get these slogans out," the driver said. "What they do with words. Take *necessary*, for instance. It means different things to different people. Like me. What's necessary to me?"

"Passengers," Parry said. "And I'll tell you what's necessary to passenges — getting where they want to go without a lot of talk."

He thought that would make the driver shut up. The driver took the taxi up to fifty and said, "I don't know. Some passengers don't mind talk."

"I do."

"Always?"

"Yes, always," Parry said. "That's why I don't have many friends."

"You know," the driver said, "it's funny about friends —"

"It's funny the way you can't take a hint," Parry said.

The driver laughed. He said, "Brother, you never drove a cab. You got no idea how lonely it gets."

"What's lonely about it? You see people."

"That's just it, brother. I see so many people, I take them to so many places. I see them getting out and going in to places. I pick up other people and I hear them talking in the back seat. I'm up here all alone and I get lonely."

"That's tough," Parry said.

"You don't believe me."

"Sure," Parry said. "I believe you. My heart goes out to you. All right, turn here, to the left. Stay on this street."

"Where we going?"

"If I give you that you'll ask me why I'm going there and what I'm going to do there. After all, a guy gets lonely driving a taxi."

"That's right, lonely," the driver said. "Lonely and smart."

Parry noticed that the driver was no longer watching the rear-view mirror. Parry said, "Smart in what way?"

"People."

64

"Talking to people?"

"And looking at people. Looking at their faces."

Parry started to shake. He glanced at his shaking hand. He measured the distance from his hand to the door handle. He said, "What about faces?"

"Well, it's funny," the driver said. "From faces I can tell what people think. I can tell what they do. Sometimes I can even tell who they are."

And now the driver again watched the rear-view mirror.

Parry reached over and put his hand on the door handle. He told himself he had to do it and do it now and do it fast. And not sit here and hope he was wrong, because he couldn't be wrong, because it was an equation again and it checked. The evening papers were out long ago and the taxi driver had to read one of those papers, had to see the picture that had to be on the front page. The taxi driver had time to read the write-up. Front-page stories were made to order for taxi drivers who didn't have time to read the back pages.

"You, for instance," the driver said.

"All right, me. What about me?"

"You're a guy with troubles."

"I don't have a trouble in the world," Parry said.

"Don't tell me, brother," the driver said. "I know. I know people. I'll tell you something else. Your trouble is women."

Parry took his hand from the door handle. It was all right. He had to stop this business of worrying about things before they happened.

He said, "Strike one. I'm happily married."

"Call it two-base hit. You're not married. But you used to be, and it wasn't happy."

"Oh, I get it. You were there. You were hiding in the closet all the time."

The driver said, "I'll tell you about her. She wasn't easy

to get along with. She wanted things. The more she got, the more she wanted. And she always got what she wanted. That's the picture."

"That's strike two."

"That's the picture," the driver said. "She never made much noise and she was always a couple steps ahead of you. Sometimes she wasn't even there at all. That gave her the upper hand, because she could keep an eye on you and you didn't know it."

"Strike three."

"Strike three my eye. You were a rubber band on her little finger."

"All right, make a left-hand turn. Go right at the next light."

"So finally—" The taxi made a wide, fast turn. "So finally it was up to your neck and you couldn't take it any more. You were tired of boxing with her—so you slugged her."

Parry was shaking again. He had his hand going toward the door handle. He said, "You know, you ought to do something with that. You could make money at carnivals."

"It's a thought."

Parry put his hand on the door handle.

The taxi made a right turn. Two neon signs flashed past, one yellow, the other violet. It was a market section. It was busy. There were people, too many people. But he didn't care. He started to work the handle.

"Yep," the driver said. "She gave you plenty of trouble. I don't blame you. I don't blame you one bit."

The handle was halfway down. Perspiration dripped onto grey worsted. The handle was almost all the way down.

"Not now," the driver said. "And not here. There's too many cops around."

CHAPTER 7

Parry let go of the handle. He sagged. He started to breathe as if he had just finished a two-mile run and the officials said it didn't count and wanted to get another race going immediately.

The driver said, "Is it far from here?"

"I'll give you five hundred dollars," Parry blurted. "I'll give you—"

"Don't give me anything," the driver said. "Just let me know where it is and I'll pick out a dark street that's empty and you can walk the rest of the way. And don't try hitting me on the head or I'll run us up on the pavement and into a wall."

Parry had his head almost to his knees. He made fists and pressed them against his forehead. He said, "The hell with it, the hell with it. Take me to a police station."

"Don't be that way. You're doing all right. You're doing fine."

"No," Parry groaned. "It's no go. It was easy for you to see. It'll be easy for others to see."

"Now that's where you're wrong," the driver said. He twisted the taxi into a sharp turn and sent it sliding down a

67

narrow street that was empty and very dark. Halfway down the street he brought the taxi to a smooth stop. He rested his arm on the back of the seat and turned and faced Parry. He said, "And here's why. I'm out of the ordinary. Not my eyes, but the way I stick things on my brain and keep them there. And the way I put things together. I get five or six little things and I put them together and I get one big thing."

"What's the difference?" Parry said. He wasn't talking to the driver. "The worst I can get is a week in solitary. And no privileges. And no chance of a parole. But there wasn't a chance anyway. They told me I was lucky I didn't get the chair. That's something I've got to remember—I'm lucky. I'll always be lucky because I didn't get the chair." He looked up and saw the driver watching him. He said, "Go on—take me to a police station."

"I don't see no sense in that," the driver said. "Unless you think you'll be happier in Quentin."

"Sure," Parry said. "I'll be happier there. That's why they send us there. To keep us happy."

The driver brought up a forearm, put most of his weight on the elbow, leaning his face against a big hand. "I got a better idea for you. Let me take you over the Bridge. You can jump off and it'll be over in no time."

"The Bridge?"

"Sure. All you gotta do is step off and you faint on the way down. It's like going to a painless dentist."

"I'm young," Parry said, again talking aloud to himself. "There's a lot of years ahead of me."

"Why spend them in Quentin?"

"What else can I do?" Parry asked.

"I want to know something," the driver said. "Did you really bump her off?"

"No."

"That's not the way I figure it," the driver said. "I figure

68

she made life miserable for you and finally you lost your head and you picked up that ash tray and slugged her. I know how it is. I live with my sister and my brother-in-law. They get along fine. They get along so fine that once he threw a bread knife at her. She ducked. And that's the way it goes. Maybe if your wife ducked there wouldn't be any trial, there wouldn't be any Quentin. But that's the way it goes. You want a smoke?"

"All right," Parry said. He accepted a cigarette and a light.

The driver filled his lungs with smoke, sent the smoke out through the side of his mouth. He said, "Let me find out something, just to see if I got it right. What was she like?"

"She was all right," Parry said. "She wasn't a bad soul. She just hated my guts. For a long time I tried to find out why. Then it got to a point where I didn't care any more. I started going out. I knew she was going out so it didn't make any difference. We hardly ever talked to each other. It was a very happy home."

"What made you marry her in the first place?"

"The old story."

"I almost got roped in a couple of times," the driver said.

"If you find the right person it's okay," Parry said.

Then they were quiet for a while. They sat there blowing smoke. After a time the driver said, "Where we going?"

"I don't know," Parry said. "What should I do?"

"You won't listen."

"I'll listen," Parry said. "I want ideas. That's what I need more than anything else. Ideas. Look, I didn't kill her. Why should I go back to San Quentin and stay there the rest of my life if I didn't kill her?"

The driver shifted his position so that he faced Parry directly. He beckoned to Parry. He said, "Come up a few inches. Let's see if he can do anything with your face."

"Who?"

"A friend of mine." The driver was studying Parry's face. The driver said, "This guy's good. He knows his stuff."

"What would he want?"

"What do you have?"

"A thousand."

"To spend?"

"No," Parry said. "A thousand's all I have."

"He'd take a couple hundred."

"What would he want afterward?"

"Not a cent. He's a friend of mine."

"What do you want?"

"Nothing." The driver got paper and a stub of pencil from an inside pocket and he was writing something.

"How long will it take?" Parry asked.

"Maybe a week if he doesn't touch your nose. I've seen him work. He's good. I don't think he'll touch your nose. I think he'll fix up you around the eyes. But you can't stay there. You got a place to stay?"

"I think so," Parry said.

The driver handed Parry a slip of paper. Parry folded it and put it in his coat pocket.

"I'll call him tonight," the driver said. "Maybe he can do it tonight. Maybe I better call him right now. You got the cash with you?"

"Yes, but I'm not sure about tonight. Let's work it this way—you call him and say there's a good chance I'll be there at two in the morning. Or better make it three. Are you sure this guy's okay?"

"He's okay as long as he knows you're okay. That good enough?"

"I'll gamble," Parry said. "How do I get in?"

"It's an old building on Post. One of them dried-up

places filled with two-by-four offices. He's got his office on the third floor. There's an alley on the left side of the building. There's a back door and he'll have it open for you. He works fast and you'll be out of there before it gets light."

"What do I do after I get out? I can't walk the streets all bandaged up."

"Don't worry about it," the driver said. "I'll be there. I know the section and I got the whole thing mapped out already. The alley cuts through to a second alley. I'll have the taxi parked there at the end of the second alley."

"Suppose he can't make it tonight."

"We'll take the chance. I think we better shove now. I don't want any cops to see me parked here. Where do we go?"

"Make a right hand turn at the end of the block," Parry said.

The taxi went down the street, made a right turn, made another right turn, then a third, then down four blocks and a left-hand turn.

"Stop alongside that apartment house," Parry said.

The taxi went halfway down the street and came to a stop.

"What'll it be?" Parry said.

"An even two bucks."

Parry handed the driver a five-dollar bill. He said, "Keep it."

The driver handed Parry a dollar bill and a dollar in silver. "You need some silver," he said. "Besides, you don't want to go throwing your money around like that. Now what's it going to be?"

"Three on the dot."

"All right. I'll call him. And you be there. And listen, keep telling yourself it'll work out okay. Keep telling yourself you don't have a thing to lose."

71

"But you," Parry said. "You've got plenty to lose. You and your friend."

"Don't worry about me and my friend," the driver said. "You just be there at three. That's all you got to worry about."

Parry opened the door and stepped out of the taxi. He walked toward the entrance of a third-rate apartment house. He heard the taxi going away and he turned and saw the tail light getting smaller in the blackness down the street.

The lobby of the apartment house was dreary. People who stayed in this place were in the forty-a-week bracket. The carpet was ready to give up and the wallpaper should have given up long ago. There were three plain chairs and a sofa sinking in the middle. There was a small table, too small for the big antique lamp that was probably taken at auction without too much bidding. Parry had been here before and every time he came here he wondered why George Fellsinger put up with it. He looked at it through the window of the door that kept him in the vestibule. He sighed and wanted to go away. There was no other place to go. He gazed down the list of tenants, came to Fellsinger and pressed the button. There wasn't any voice arrangement. There wasn't any response to the first press. Parry pressed again. There wasn't any response. Maybe the Bridge was better after all. It didn't pay to keep up with this, all this vacuum in the stomach, going around, going up to his brain and going back to his stomach and coming up again and eating away at his heart. He pressed the button again, and this time he got a buzz and he opened the door, quickly crossed the lobby, saw that the elevator was right there waiting for him. Maybe the police were waiting upstairs. Maybe they weren't.

The elevator took him to the fourth floor. He hurried down the corridor, knocked on the door of Fellsinger's

72

apartment.

The door opened. Parry stepped into the apartment. The door closed. George Fellsinger folded his arms and leaned against the door and said, "Jesus Christ."

George Fellsinger was thirty-six and losing his blonde hair. He was five nine and he had the kind of build they show in the muscle development ads, the kind of build a man has before he sends the coupon away and gets the miracle machine. Fellsinger had blue eyes that were more water than blue and the frayed collar of his starched white shirt was open at the throat.

The apartment was just like Fellsinger. It consisted of a room and a bath and a kitchenette. The davenport was set with pillow and sheets and there were six ash trays stocked with stubs, a magazine on the floor, an empty ginger-ale bottle resting on the magazine. Parry knew Fellsinger had fallen asleep on the davenport after having finished the magazine and the ginger ale and the cigarettes. There was a trumpet on one of two chairs.

"Jesus Christ," Fellsinger said again.

"How've you been, George?"

"I've been all right. Jesus, Vincent, I never expected anything like this—" Fellsinger ran to a small table, opened a drawer, took out a carton of cigarettes. With a thumbnail he slit the carton, extracted a pack, and with the same thumbnail he opened the pack, with the same thumbnail got a match lit. He ignited Parry's cigarette, ignited his own and then went back to the door and leaned against it.

"You saw the papers?"

"Sure," Fellsinger said. "And I couldn't believe it. And I can't believe this."

"There's no getting away from it, George. I'm here. This is really me."

"In that brand-new suit?"

73

Parry explained the suit. From the suit he went back to the road, told Fellsinger how she had picked him up, told Fellsinger everything.

"You can't work it that way," Fellsinger said. "What you've got to do is take yourself out of town. Out of the state. Out of the country."

"That's for later. What I need now is a new face."

"He'll ruin you. I tell you, Vince, you're working it wrong. Every minute you waste in town is—"

"Look, George, you said I was innocent. You always kept saying that. Do you still believe it?"

"Of course. It was an accident. Nobody killed her."

"All right, then. Do you want to help me?"

"Of course I want to help you. Anything, Vince. Anything I can do. For Christ's sake—"

"Look, George, have there been any big changes in your life since they put me away?"

"I don't know what you mean."

"I mean, you never used to have any visitors. You were always alone up here. Is it still that way?"

"Yes. I lead a miserable life, Vince. You know that. You know I have nobody. You were my only friend." A suggestion of tears appeared in Fellsinger's eyes.

Parry didn't notice the tears. He said, "I'm mighty glad nobody comes up here. That'll make it easy. And it won't be more than a week. Do it for me, George. That's all I'm asking. Just let me stay here for a week."

"Vince, you can stay here for a year, for ten years. But that's not the point. You said she gave you money. That's half the battle already. With money you can travel. Here you'll only run into the police. Maybe even now—"

"I can't travel with this face. It needs to be changed. I'm going there tonight. Maybe the police will be here when I get back. Maybe not. It's fifty-fifty."

Fellsinger took a key case from the back pocket of his

74

trousers. He unringed a key and handed it to Parry. "It's good for both doors," he said. "I still think you're working it wrong, Vince."

"Got anything to drink?"

"Some rum. It's awful stuff, but that's all I can get these days."

"Rum. Anything."

Fellsinger went into the kitchen, came out with a bottle of rum and two water glasses. He half filled both glasses.

They stood facing each other, gulping the rum.

"I still can't believe it," Fellsinger said.

"I was lucky," Parry said. "I got breaks. If I had planned it for a year it couldn't have worked out any better. The truck was right where I wanted it to be. The guards were nowhere around. It was all luck."

"And that girl," Fellsinger said.

Parry started to say something, then found his lips were closed, found the words were crumbling up and becoming nothing. He didn't want to talk about her. He was sorry he had told Fellsinger about her. He couldn't understand why he had told Fellsinger everything, even her name and her address and even the number of her apartment. He was very sorry he had done that but he didn't know why he was sorry. He knew only that now and from now on he didn't want to talk about her, he didn't want to think about her.

Fellsinger made himself horizontal on the davenport. He finished the rum in his glass, got the glass half filled again. Parry brought a chair toward the davenport and sat down.

"And Madge Rapf," Fellsinger said. "You sure that's who it was?"

"That's who it was."

"All my life I've tried to keep from hating people," Fellsinger said. "That's one of the people I hate. I remember once I was at your apartment with you and Gert, and Madge walked in. I saw the way she was looking at you. I remember what I was thinking. That she was out to get you and once she had you she'd rip you apart and throw the pieces away. Then she'd go out and look for the pieces and put them together and rip you apart again. That's Madge Rapf. And how come she's connected with this Janney girl? What takes place there?"

Parry thought he had already told Fellsinger what took place there. Wondering why he kept it back now, he said, "I don't know."

"Sure you don't know?"

"George, I've told you everything, I'm depending on you now. I wouldn't keep anything from you."

Fellsinger took a long gulp of rum. He said, "I wish I could sleep with Madge Rapf."

"Are you out of your mind?"

"You don't get me," Fellsinger said. "I wish I could sleep with her provided I was sure she talked in her sleep. I think she'd say the things I want her to say. I think she'd admit Gert never made that dying statement. Jesus Christ, if we could only prove that was a frame."

"I don't think it was a frame," Parry said. "I think Madge was telling the truth."

"Maybe she thought she was telling the truth. Maybe she drilled it into herself that Gert really said that. People like Madge make a habit of that sort of thing. It becomes part of their make-up."

"Gert hated me."

"Gert didn't hate you. Gert just didn't care for you. There's a difference. Gert would have walked out on you only she had no one else to go to. No one."

"There were others."

"They weren't permanent. She would have walked out if she could have found something permanent. And she wouldn't frame you, Vince. She was no prize package, but she wouldn't frame you. Madge framed you. Madge

76

wanted to hook you. When she couldn't hook you one way, she hooked you another way. Madge is a fine girl."

"Maybe one of these days she'll get run over by an automobile."

"It's something to pray for," Fellsinger said. He took a thick watch from the small top pocket of his trousers. "What's your schedule?"

"I want to be there at three."

"Plenty of time," Fellsinger said.

"How's the job going?"

"The same job," Fellsinger said. "The same rotten routine. Sometimes I feel it getting the best of me. Last week I asked for a raise and Wolcott laughed in my face. I wanted to spit in his and walk out. One of these days I'm going to do just that. I can't stand Wolcott. I can't stand anything about that place. Thirty-five dollars a week."

"What are you kicking about? That's a marvelous salary."

"I talked to my doctor a few months ago. I asked him if I could stand a manual job. He said the only kind of job I could stand was a job where I sit in one place all day and don't use my muscles. I had no idea I was in such awful shape. He gave me a list of rules to follow, diet and cigarettes and liquor and all that. Rather than follow those rules I'd throw myself into the Bay."

"You mean jump off the Bridge?"

"What?"

"Nothing."

"Not nothing. Something. You've been thinking in terms of the Bridge. You got to get rid of that, Vince. That's no good."

"I'm all right. And everything's going to be all right. With a new face I won't need to worry. At least I won't need to worry so much. As long as I'm careful, as long as I keep my wits about me, as long as I have something to

77

hold on to I'll be all right."

They sat there talking about themselves, the things that had once amounted to something in common. Fellsinger's amateur status with the trumpet. Fellsinger's refusal to go professional. Fellsinger's ideas in regard to sincere jazz. Fellsinger's interest in higher mathematics, and his lack of real ability with higher mathematics, and his feeling that if he had real ability he could make a lot of money in investment securities. Fellsinger's lack of real ability with anything. Parry's claim that Fellsinger had real ability with something and as soon as he found that something he would start getting somewhere. Their vacation at Lake Tahoe a few years back. Fishing at Tahoe and the two girls from Nevada who wanted to learn how to fish. Empty bottles of gin all over the cabin. What a wonderful two weeks it had been, and how they agreed that next summer they would be there again at Tahoe. But they weren't there the next summer because Parry was married that next summer and Gert wanted a honeymoon in Oregon. She wanted to see Crater Lake National Park. She was interested in mineralogy. She collected stones. She claimed there was flame opal to be found in Crater Lake National Park. She liked opal, the flame opal, the white opal with flames of green and orange writhing under the glistening white. She was always asking Parry to get her something in the way of flame opal. He couldn't afford flame opal but he got her a stone anyway. He went to a credit jewelry store downtown and said he wanted a flame-opal ring. They said they didn't have any flame opal in stock but if he came back in a few days they would have something. He didn't tell Gert about it. He wanted to surprise her. She would have a birthday in four days and he would have that flame opal in three. When he went back to the credit jewelry store they had the flame opal, a fairly large stone set in white gold with a small diamond on each side. They wanted nine hundred dollars. Parry had figured on about four hundred dollars and he was telling himself his only move was to turn and walk out of the store. Then he was thinking the flame opal would make Gert very happy. She hadn't found any flame opal in Crater Lake National Park. It ruined the honeymoon. She was always saying how badly she wanted flame opal. Parry made a down payment of three hundred dollars, which reduced his bank account to one hundred dollars. He told them to wrap the ring nicely. He took the ring home and on the following day, which was Gert's birthday, he presented her with the flame opal. She snatched it out of his hand. She broke a fingernail tearing off the wrapping. Parry was in the room but Gert was all alone in the room with her flame opal and she had a magnifying glass and she studied the stone for twenty minutes. Then when she saw Parry was there she asked him how much he had paid for the stone. He told her. She asked him where he had bought the stone. He told her. She started to carry on. She said he didn't have any sense. She said the credit jewelry store was a gyp point and anybody with half a brain wouldn't put out nine hundred dollars for a flame opal in a place of that sort. She told him to take the ring back and demand his money. She said the flame opal was full of flaws and the diamond were chips and at the very most the ring was worth two hundred dollars. She hopped up and down and made a lot of noise. He asked her to quiet down. She threw the ring at him and it hit him in the face and cut his cheek. Gert started to sob and yell at the same time and Parry begged her to quiet down. He said he would take back the ring and try to regain his down payment. She laughed at him. On the following day he took the ring back but they wouldn't return the down payment. When he became insistent they told him to get a lawyer. He said the ring wasn't worth nine hundred dollars. They told him to go get a lawyer. He walked out of the store and he was very weary and he knew he was out three hundred dollars. He wanted to go home and tell Gert he had regained the three hundred and put it back in the bank. He knew that wouldn't work. He had never been much good at putting a lie across. He told himself Gert was right. He didn't have any sense. He should have used his head and taken her with him when he went to purchase her birthday gift. She was absolutely right. He didn't have any sense. It was for his own good she had carried on like that. She wanted him to be something, not a nothing. She wanted him to be something she could respect. He put his hand to the cut on his cheek. She hadn't meant to do that. She hadn't meant to hurt him. It was for his own good. Maybe this would be the beginning of a change in his life. Maybe from here on he would start to use his head and make something of himself, climb out of that thirty-five-a-week rut in the investment security house. Maybe this was all for the best. He went to the bank and took out fifty of the remaining hundred. He went into a large, dignified jewelry store and asked if they had anything in the way of flame opal. A man wearing white and black and grey looked Parry up and down and said they didn't have anything under six hundred dollars. Parry walked out of the store. He went into another store ands they didn't have anything under seven hundred dollars. He went into a third store and a fourth and a fifth. He was forty minutes past his lunch hour and he hadn't eaten yet and he was getting a fierce headache. He made up his mind he wouldn't go back to the office until he had a flame opal for his wife. He went into a sixth store. A seventh and an eighth. The headache was awful. He went into the ninth store and it was a small establishment that seemed sincere, that also seemed as if it was having a hard time staying on its feet. A man well past seventy showed Parry a ring set with a rather small flame opal, a sterling silver setting. The ring looked as if it had been in the store since the store was founded, and the store looked as if it had been founded a hundred years ago. But it was a flame opal and Gert wanted a flame opal, and when the man said $97.50 it became a sale. Parry threw a milkshake down his throat and sprinted back to the office. When he arrived at the office the headache was taking his head apart and Wolcott was telling him this sort of thing would never do, and besides his work lately had been anything but satisfactory, and he had better wise up to himself before he found himself out on the street looking for another job. When Parry got home that night he tried to kiss Gert but she turned away from him. He handed her the small package and said happy birthday. She opened the small package and looked at the small flame opal. She looked at it for a while and then she let it fall to the floor. She put on her hat and coat. Parry asked her where she was going. She didn't answer. She walked out of the apartment. Parry heard the door slamming shut. He reached down, picked up the ring. He looked at the closed door, then looked at the flame opal, then looked at the closed door and then looked at the flame opal.

CHAPTER 8

Fellsinger tilted the bottle, poured rum into the two glasses.

"What time is it?" Parry asked.

Fellsinger glanced at his wrist watch. "One thirty."

"I better get going." Parry downed the rum.

"When will you be back?"

"I'd say around five or five thirty." Parry reached in his coat pocket, took out the key Fellsinger had given him. "Got one for yourself?"

"Yes. I've always kept two keys, although I don't know why."

"Should I wake you up when I come in?" Parry asked.

Fellsinger grinned. "Do that. I want to see what you look like."

"I'll be all bandaged up. I'll be a mess."

"Wake me up anyway," Fellsinger said.

"I hate to walk out of here," Parry said. "I hate to go down that elevator and out on that street."

"You don't need to go. You can stay here. I'm telling you you're better off if you stay. Once you walk out—"

"No. I'll have to do it sooner or later and I might as well

do it now. Can you spare a pack of cigarettes?"

"Absolutely not." Fellsinger took a pack from the carton, took another pack and handed the two packs to Parry. He was up from the davenport as Parry got up from the chair. He hit Parry on the shoulder and said, "For Christ's sake, Vince—be careful."

"Careful," Parry said. "Careful and lucky. That's what it's got to be. You better go to sleep now, George. You got a day of work ahead of you tomorrow."

"Be careful, Vince, will you?" Fellsinger walked Parry to the door. He put his hand on the knob. He tried to keep his hand steady but his hand shook. He said, "Be careful, Vince."

Parry opened the door and went down the corridor. He pressed the elevator button and stood there waiting. The elevator came up for him and just before he stepped in he turned and saw Fellsinger standing beside the open door. Fellsinger was smiling. Fellsinger was giving him a little wave of encouragement. He smiled and waved back and entered the elevator. As the elevator took him down he extracted the folded slip of paper from his coat pocket. He looked at the name, *Walter Coley*, and the address on Post street, and *third floor—room 303*. The elevator came to a stop and Parry walked out of the apartment house, walked for two blocks and saw a wide street that had car tracks. A streetcar was approaching but he knew he couldn't take a streetcar. He had to depend on another taxi. He opened one of the cigarette packs, realized he had no matches, put the pack back in his pocket. He looked up and down the street and there was nothing resembling a taxi. He walked down the wide street, telling himself that he needed a smoke, needed it badly. He walked into a small confectionery store. There was an old woman behind the counter.

"A book of matches," Parry said.

The old woman put two books of matches on the counter and said, "A penny. Anything else?"

"No," Parry said. He was handling some of the silver the taxi driver had given him. The old woman was looking at him. He put a nickel on the counter.

"You don't have any pennies?" the old woman said.

He didn't like the way she was looking at him. She seemed to be examining his face. Then she was turning her head slowly and her eyes were going to another part of the store and Parry's eyes went along with her eyes, following her eyes, then frantically leaping ahead of her eyes and getting there first, getting to the stack of newspapers beside a candy counter, getting to the front page and the big photograph of Vincent Parry on the front page. Automatically he sucked in his cheeks and frowned and tried to change the set of his face, and as the eyes of the old woman came back to his face he made an abrupt turn and he was going out of the store.

"You got change coming," the old woman said.

Parry was out of the store and walking fast down the street. As he neared the end of the block he started to run. He had a picture of the old woman at a telephone, a picture of a police sergeant at the other end of the line. He ran fast, and faster, as fast as he could go. The empty pavement went sliding toward him, dim white in the lateness of empty night, then gave way to black street. In the middle of the street he told himself he ought to turn here, he ought to get off the wide street. As he turned he saw two headlights coming at him and he heard a horn honking and he tried to get out of the way. The horn honked again and with the horn Parry heard the brakes fighting with momentum, fighting with the street and trying to do something for him. Then the automobile hit him, and as he went down under the bumper, going around in the big

84

circle that was a preliminary to sleep, he told himself this was the first time in his life he had ever been hit by an automobile.

CHAPTER 9

Someone was saying, "—turned and came right at me."

Someone else said, "You should have full control of your car at all times. Your speed—"

"Officer, I swear I wasn't doing more than twenty-five."

"That's what you say. Now we'll see what he has to say. He's coming to."

Parry raised his head, lifted himself on his elbows. He saw the big face in front of his own face, the shield on the cap, the bright buttons on the coat. There were other faces surrounding the big face but he wasn't paying attention to them. He kept staring at the big face of the policeman.

Someone was saying, "Officer, I should drop down dead if I was doing more than twenty-five. As true as there's—"

"All right, save that for later," the policeman said.

Parry said, "I'm all right, officer." He stood up. There was a pain in the back of his head. There was a pain in his right knee. He put a hand to the back of his head and felt the bump. He took a couple of steps forward and people were stepping back to give him room.

The policeman had a long rounded nose and a rounded chin. The policeman put a huge arm around Parry's middle and said, "Sure you're all right?"

"Perfectly sure," Parry said, squirming away from the policeman's arm. "Just had the wind knocked out of me."

"Thank God," someone said, and Parry turned and saw a little man who had a bald head and a moustache that was too big for his little face.

The policeman faced the little man and said, "Cards."

"Sure, officer. Right here." The little man tussled with a back pocket and took out a wallet. It was an overloaded wallet and as the little man hurried to open it a collection of cards and papers fluttered out and showered to the street.

Parry said, "I'm all right, officer. No damage at all."

"He hit you, didn't he?" the policeman said.

The little man was on his knees, picking up the papers and cards. The little man looked up and said, "I'm telling you, officer, I wasn't doing more than—"

"Aw, keep quiet, will ya?" the policeman said impatiently. "All I want from you is your cards."

"Yes, sir," the little man said. He went on picking up the papers and cards.

Someone said, "Better call an ambulance."

"I don't need an ambulance," Parry said. He wondered if there was a chance to make a break. He estimated nine people in this bunch. Out of nine maybe there were none who could run as fast as he. Undoubtedly he could run faster than the big policeman.

"Got any pain?" the policeman said.

"None at all," Parry said. "I'm perfectly all right."

"You sure?" the policeman said.

The little man was up with the papers and cards, saying, "If he says he's all right then he must be all right."

Turning to the little man, the policeman said, "What are you, master of ceremonies? Let's see those cards."

"Yes, sir," the little man said. He was extending cards. "My driver's license, and here's my owner's—"

87

"All right, I got eyes," the policeman said. He studied the cards. He looked at the little man.

Parry said, "It wasn't his fault, officer. I ran right in front of his car."

"That's right, officer," the little man said. "That's just the way it was. I was—"

"Let's take this step by step," the policeman said. He pushed the cap back on his head. He looked at Parry. "You say it wasn't his fault?"

"That's right. It wasn't his fault at all."

"That's right, officer," the little man said. "I was—"

"Now look, Max—" the policeman pushed the cap forward again. "I'm in charge of this deal and it's going to be handled my way. Is that clear, Max?"

"Sure, officer," the little man said. "You're in charge. Anything you say goes. All I want to do is—"

"Max," the policeman said, "all you want to do is keep that mouth of yours quiet so's I can get this matter straightened out." He turned to Parry. "Now look, mister, are you sure you're all right?"

Someone said, "I'd call an ambulance. If it's a skull fracture—"

"It ain't a skull fracture," the little man said loudly.

"How do you know it ain't?" the other man said.

The little man faced the big policeman and gestured toward Parry. He said, "The man's got a bump on the head and already they got him dead and buried."

"If it was up to me I'd get an ambulance," the other man said.

The policeman turned and faced the other man. The policeman said, "It ain't up to you. I'm in charge here, unless you want to argue about it."

"I'm not arguing about anything," the other man said aggressively. "All I say is you ought to get an ambulance."

The policeman took a step forward while pointing back to Parry and saying, "Do you know that man?"

Parry was telling himself all he had to do was get past the policeman because there was a gap to the left of the policeman and if he could get through the gap he would be on his way.

The other man was saying, "No."

"All right then," the policeman said. "If you don't know him it ain't none of your business."

"I'm a citizen," the other man said. "I've lived in this city for thirty-seven years."

"I don't care if you were one of the founders," the policeman said.

"I've got certain privileges," the other man said.

The policeman took another step forward. He said, "Look, friend, it's a late hour. Why don't you go home and get a good night's rest?"

It got a few laughs. The man didn't like being laughed at. He pointed a long arm at Parry. He said, "That man—" and Parry was all set to run "—that man might have a skull fracture. And I say it's your official duty, as a sworn servant of the law, to protect the citizens of this city. It is your official duty to call an ambulance."

"I said I was all right," Parry said.

The policeman turned to Parry and said, "Mister, what's your name?"

Parry looked at the policeman. He said, "Studebaker."

"What's that again?"

"Studebaker," Parry said. "George Studebaker."

"Does it make any difference what his name is?" the little man said. "If he's not going to prefer charges—"

"God damn it, I'm handling this," the policeman said.

"You're handling it all wrong," said the man who had lived in San Francisco thirty-seven years.

"Now listen here, you," the policeman said. He pushed the cap back on his head. "You keep that up and I'll run you in for interfering with an officer in the performance of his duty."

"You won't do anything of the sort," the man said. "I'm a citizen. I'm a respectable member of this community. I've got a clean record and I own my own home. I've got a wife and four children. I've worked in the same plant for thirty-two years."

"And never been late or absent," someone said.

"Absent once," the man said. "I fell down a flight of stairs and broke my left leg."

"That's too bad," the policeman said. "How's the leg now?"

It's all right now."

"That's fine," the policeman said. "That means you can walk. So go ahead and walk."

"Sure," the little man said, coming up to stand beside the policeman. "Go home already."

"Nobody asked you," the other man said. "You're just one of these wise little Jews."

The little man was stiff for a moment, then he bent back, like a strip of flexible steel, and sprang forward with both fists slashing at the other man's face, but before he could reach the other man the policeman grabbed him. He tried to get away from the policeman. He tried to get to the other man and he said, "You can't talk like that any more. We don't take it any more. We're through taking it. If my boy in the South Pacific was here now he'd tear you apart with his bare hands. You got to realize you can't talk like that any more. Let go of me, officer. I won't let him get away with that. I won't let any of them get away with that. I don't care if they're eight feet tall—"

"All right, Max," the policeman said soothingly. "Take it easy."

"We don't take it easy any more," the little man said. "We don't let them talk like that any more."

The crowd was looking at the other man. The other man was backing away. The policeman looked at the other man and said, "That's right, take a walk, because I got a good mind to let Max loose, and once he gets loose you're gonna regret the whole thing. It happens I also had a boy in the South Pacific."

The man who had lived in San Francisco for thirty-seven years was backing away, gradually turning, so that at last he had his back to the crowd and was walking quickly down the street.

"Now I don't care what happens," the little man said. His whole body was shaking. "You can call the ambulance, you can call the wagon. I don't care what you do. I don't care."

Someone said, "Why don't we justs break it up already?"

The policeman pushed the cap farther back on his head, turned to Parry and said, "Look, Studebaker, are you sure you're all right?"

"I'm absolutely sure, officer," Parry said. "You'd be doing me a favor if you let it ride."

The policeman pushed the cap farther back on his head, stood there with uncertainty all over his face, rubbed a big hand across his big chin. Then he pushed the cap forward on his head, glared at the crowd and said, "All right, let's break it up."

The crowd moved back as the policeman walked forward. The crowd radiated.

Parry told himself to wait, to hold it until the policeman crossed the street. The little man came over to Parry and said, "Thanks, mister. You could have said it was my fault."

"It's all right," Parry said. He was watching the policeman.

"Maybe you ought to see a doctor after all," the little man said. "Can I take you any place?"

"No," Parry said. "Thanks anyway. Wait. You going toward Post?"

"Sure," the little man said. "I'm not going there but I'll

go there anyway. Any place you want to go."

They stepped into the car. Both doors closed. The little man was still shaking and he stalled the car twice before he really got it going. The car made a turn. Parry took out a pack of cigarettes.

"Smoke?"

"Thanks," the little man said. "I need it."

Parry gave him a light, lit his own, leaned back and watched the street lamps parading quickly toward the car.

"Sometimes I just get burned up," the little man said.

"I know."

"I get so burned up I don't know what I'm doing," the little man said. "And it's not good for me. I got high blood pressure. I've had it for years."

Parry was watching the rear-view mirror.

The little man was taking something from his pocket.

Parry tugged hard at the cigarette and wondered if the single light he saw back there was the headlamp of a motorcycle.

"Here, take this," the little man said, handing Parry a card. "I'm nobody important, but any time I can do you a favor—"

Parry looked at the card. Glow from the street lamps showed him *Max Weinstock, Upholsterer.*

"Sure you feel all right?" the little man said.

"I'm fine," Parry said. "I wasn't hurt at all."

"But maybe you should see a doctor just to make sure."

"No, I'm all right," Parry said.

The little man looked at him.

Parry looked at the rear-view mirror.

The car made another turn, stopped for a light, went down three blocks, stopped for another light, made another turn and the little man said, "Whereabouts on Post?"

Parry took the folded slip of paper from his pocket, studied it for a few moments. He directed the little man to let him off at a street that was one block away from the address on the paper.

The car made another turn, going left on Post.

"Do you have the time?" Parry said, forgetting the watch on his wrist.

The little man glanced at a wrist watch. "Two-thirty."

"Too early," Parry said.

"Early?"

"Nothing," Parry said. "I was just thinking."

The little man was looking at him. As the car stopped for another light the little man leaned forward slightly so he could get a better look at Parry's face. Parry took out the pack, lit another cigarette, sustaining the match and holding his left hand in front of the left side of his face. Glancing sideways, he knew the little man was still looking at him. He had a feeling it was going to happen now, while they were waiting for this light to change. He told himself Post was reasonably empty and he could handle the little man as he had handled Studebaker. The little man was still looking at him and now he had his cigarette going and the match was going to burn his fingers. He blew out the match, his hand came down. The little man was still looking at him. Parry's teeth clicked, his head turned mechanically, he stared at the little man, his stare went past the eyes of the little man and he was staring at a police squad car parked there beside the little man's car.

The light changed. The police squad car went forward.

"The light changed," Parry said.

The little man turned and looked at the light. He made no move to get the car going.

"The light changed," Parry said.

"Yes," the little man said. "I know." He made no move to get the car going.

"What's the matter?" Parry said.

The little man looked at him.

"Can't we get started?" Parry said.

The little man was leaning back now, his head was down, he was looking at nothing.

"Won't the car go?" Parry said.

"The car's all right," the little man said.

"Then what's the matter?" Parry said. "Why are we standing here?"

The little man looked at Parry. The little man said nothing.

"I don't get you," Parry said. He looked at the rear-view mirror. He put fingers on the door handle. He said, "We can't stay here in the middle of the street. We're blocking traffic."

"There's no traffic," the little man said. It was under a whisper.

"Well, why don't we move?" Parry said. He gripped the door handle.

The little man said nothing. He was leaning back again. His head was down again. He was looking at nothing again.

"What's the matter with you?" Parry said. "Are you sick or something?"

"I'm not sick." It was way under a whisper.

"Then what's the matter? What are you sitting there like that for? What's wrong with you? What are you doing sitting there like that? What are you doing? Answer me, what are you doing? What are you doing?"

The little man raised his head slowly and he was gazing straight ahead and still he looked at nothing. Then he said, "I'm thinking."

CHAPTER 10

The light changed again.

Parry tried to put pressure on the door handle. He couldn't collect any pressure.

The motor stopped.

Parry wanted to hear the motor going. He said, "Start the car."

The little man pressed his foot against the starter. The car jumped forward and stalled. The little man started the motor again, the car inched forward.

"Don't go against the light," Parry said. "Wait for the light to change."

The little man crossed his arms on the steering wheel, leaned his head on his arms. Parry got some pressure on the door handle, got the door handle moving, then took his hand away, wondered why he was taking his hand away, wondered why he was staying in the car.

The light changed.

"All right," Parry said. "The light changed. Let's go."

The little man brought his head up, looked at the light, looked at Parry. Then he had the car in first gear and he was letting the clutch out. He was driving the car across the intersection, turning the wheel slowly, bringing the car to a stop at the curb.

Again Parry had his fingers on the door handle. He looked at the little man and said, "What are we stopping for?"

"Let me look at you," the little man said.

"What?"

"Let me take a good look at you."

They faced each other and Parry had his right hand hardening slowly, shaping a fist. And the fist trembled. He wondered if he had the strength to go through with it.

The little man said, "Are you sure you're all right?"

"I didn't do it," Parry said. "I didn't do it and I won't go back."

"You won't go back where?"

"I won't go back."

The little man put a hand to his forehead, rubbed his forehead, rubbed his eyes as if he had a headache. He said, "Nobody claimed it was your fault. It was just one of those things. It was an accident."

"That's right," Parry said. "That's what I told them. It was an accident."

The little man brought his face closer to Parry's face and said, "You don't look so good to me."

Parry was trying to make his way through a huge barrel that rolled fast and messed up his footing. He heard himself saying, "What are you going to do about it?"

And he heard the little man saying, "I think you better let me take you to a hospital."

The barrel stopped rolling. Parry said, "Stop worrying about it."

"I can't help worrying," the little man said. "Will you do me a favor? Will you let a doctor look you over?"

Parry was working the door handle. He had it down now and he was getting the door open. He said, "I'll do that," and then the door was open and he was out of the car, the door was closed again, the light was changing and the car was going away from him.

He got his legs working. The pain in his head was going away, and he found it easy to breathe, easy to walk, easy to think. The whole thing was beginning to lean toward his side of it. He really had a grip on it now and it was going along with him. Everything was going along. And everybody, so far. Beginning with Studebaker, although with Studebaker it was involuntary. With the policeman who had looked under the blanket it was sheer carelessness. With Irene it was her own choice and the reason for that choice was an immense question mark despite the things she had told him. With the taxi driver it was human kindness. With George Fellsinger it was friendship. With the old woman in the candy store it was bad eyesight, because if her eyes were halfway decent she would have checked his face with that picture on the front page. And he knew she hadn't checked it, because if she had it would have brought a parade of police cars to the scene of the accident a few blocks away from the candy store. With Max it was as Max had put, just one of those things. He had to forget about it, because it didn't matter now and he had to check off everything that didn't matter. He remembered his wrist watch and the hands showed him 2:55.

The slip of paper came out of his pocket and he glanced at the address, pushed the paper back in his pocket and walked faster. In a few minutes he was there. He looked up along the windows of a dilapidated four-story building. The windows were dark, except for reflected light from dim street lamps that showed dirt on the glass. The alley bordering the building was very black and waiting for him. He walked down the alley.

The alley branched off to the right at the rear of the building. He went that way, came to the door. He touched the door. He touched the knob. He handled the knob, turned it. He opened the door.

He went in and closed the door. Weak greenish light

from one of the upper floors came staggering down a narrow stairway. The place was very old and very neglected. Parry went over to the stairway and let some of the greenish light get on the wrist-watch dial. The hands said 2:59. He was on time. He was all set. He started up the stairway.

The greenish light didn't come from the first floor. It didn't come from the second floor. It came from a hanging bulb on the third floor, and it illuminated several of the mottled glass panels in splintered doors. There was an advertising specialty company and a firm of mystic book publishers and an outfit that called itself Excelsior Enterprises. Parry walked down the corridor. He came to a glass panel that had the words—*Walter Coley.* And underneath—*Plastic Specialist.* A suggestion of yellow glow came from the other side of the glass.

Parry tapped fingers against the glass.

There were footsteps from inside, a trading of voices. Then more footsteps, and then the door opened, and the taxi driver stood there. The taxi driver had a half-smoked cigar between his teeth.

"How's it going?" the taxi driver said.

"It's going all right," Parry said.

The taxi driver stepped back. Parry walked in and the taxi driver closed the door. This room was trying to be a waiting room. It was nothing more than an old room with a few chairs and an old rug and sick wallpaper. The yellow glow came from the other room. The taxi driver went forward, opened the door leading to the other room, walked in and Parry followed.

It was another old room. It was very small. There was a single secondhand barber's chair from about fifteen years back. There was a big sink and three glass cabinets stocked with scissors, knives, forceps and other instruments designed to get through flesh. There was a short thin man, seventy if he was a day, and his hair was white as hair can

98

be, and his skin was white kidskin, and his eyes were a very pale blue. He wore a white sport shirt, open at the throat, and white cotton trousers held up by a white belt. He looked at Parry's face and then he looked at the taxi driver.

The taxi driver chewed on the cigar and said, "Well, Walt—what do you think?"

Coley put a hand to the side of his jaw, supported his elbow with the other hand. He got his eyes on Parry's face again and he said, "Around the eyes, mostly. And the mouth. And the cheeks. I'm going to leave the nose alone. It's a nice nose. It would be a shame to break it."

"Will I need to come back again?" Parry asked.

"No. I wouldn't want you to come back again anyway. I'm taking a big enough chance as it is." He turned to the taxi driver. He said, "Sam, I won't need you in here. Go into the other room and read a magazine."

The taxi driver walked out and closed the door.

Coley pointed to the ancient barber's chair. Parry sat down in it and Coley began working a pedal and the chair began going down. The chair went down to a shallow oblique and Coley pulled a lamp toward the chair, aimed the lamp at Parry's face and tugged at a short chain. The lamp stabbed a pearly ray at Parry's face.

Parry closed his eyes. The towel-covered headrest felt too hard against his skull. The chair was uncomfortable. He felt as if he was on a rack. He heard water running and he opened his eyes and saw Coley standing at the sink and working up a lather on white hands. Coley stood there at the sink for fully five minutes. Then he waved his hands to get some of the water off and he held his hands up in the air with the fingers drooping toward him as he came back to the chair and looked at Parry's face.

"Will it take long?" Parry said.

"Ninety minutes," Coley said. "No more."

"I thought it took much longer than that," Parry said.

Coley bent lower to study Parry's face and said, "I have

my own method. I perfected it twelve years ago. It's based on the idea of calling a spade a spade. I don't monkey around. You have the money?"

"Yes."

"Sam said you can afford two hundred dollars."

"You want it now?"

Coley nodded. Parry took bills from his pocket, selected two one-hundred dollar bills, placed them on the top of a cabinet neighboring the chair. Coley looked at the money. Then he looked at Parry's face.

Parry said, "I'm a coward. I don't like pain."

"We're all cowards," Coley said. "There's no such thing as courage. There's only fear. A fear of getting hurt and a fear of dying. That's why the human race has lasted so long. You won't have any pain with this. I'm going to freeze your face. Do you want to see yourself now?"

"Yes," Parry said.

"Sit up and take a look in that mirror." Coley pointed to a mirror that topped one of the cabinets.

Parry looked at himself.

"It's a fairly good face," Coley said. "It'll be even better when I'm done with it. And it'll be very different."

Parry relaxed in the chair. He closed his eyes again. He heard water running. He didn't open his eyes. He heard the sound of metal getting moved around, the sound of a cabinet drawer opening and shutting, the clink of steel against steel, the water running again. He kept his eyes closed. Then things were happening to his face. Some kind of oil was getting rubbed into his face, rubbed in thoroughly all over his face and then wiped off thoroughly. He smelled alcohol, felt the alcohol being dabbed onto his face. Then water running again. More clinking of steel, more cabinet drawers in action. He tried to make himself comfortable in the chair. He decided it was impossible for Coley to do this job in ninety minutes. He decided it was impossible for Coley to change the face so that people

100

wouldn't recognize it as belonging to Vincent Parry. He decided there wasn't any sense to this, and the only thing he would get out of it was something horrible happening to his face and he would be a freak for the rest of his life. He wondered how many faces Coley had ruined. He decided his face was going to look horrible but people would recognize him anyway and he wondered what he was doing up here in this quack set-up in San Francisco when he should be riding far away from San Francisco. He decided his only move was to jump out of the chair and run out of the office and keep on running.

He stayed there in the chair. He felt a needle going into his face. Then it went into his face again in another place. It kept jabbing deep into his face. His face began to feel odd. Metal was coming up against the flesh, pressing into the flesh, cutting into the flesh. There was no pain, there was no sensation except the metal going into his flesh. Different shapes of metal. He couldn't understand why he preferred to keep his eyes closed while this was going on.

It went on. With every minute that passed something new was happening to his face. Gradually he became accustomed to it—the entrance of steel into his flesh. He had the feeling he had gone through this sort of thing many times before. Now he was beginning to get some comfort out of the chair and there was a somewhat luxurious heaviness in his head and it became heavier and heavier and he knew he was falling asleep. He didn't mind. The manipulation of steel against his face and into his face took on a rhythm that mixed with the heaviness and formed a big, heavy ball that rolled down and rolled up and took him along with it, first on the top of it, on the outside, then getting him inside, rolling him around as it went up and down on its rolling path. And he was asleep.

He had a dream.

He dreamed he was a boy again in Maricopa, Arizona. A boy of fifteen running along a blackened street. He was

101

running alone and eventually he came to a place where a woman was performing on a trapeze. From neck to ankles the woman was garbed in a skin-tight costume of bright orange satin. The woman's hair was darkish orange. The woman had drab brown eyes and her skin was tanned. It was the artificial tan that came from a violet-ray lamp. The woman was about five feet four inches tall and she was very thin and she was not at all pretty but there was nothing in her face to suggest ugliness. It was just that she was not a pretty woman. But she was a wonderful acrobat. She smiled at him. She took the trapeze way up high and sailed away from it. She described three slow somersaults going backwards, going up, going over and coming down on the trapeze again as it whizzed back. Elephants in the three rings far below lifted their trunks and lifted their eyes and watched her admiringly. The trapeze whizzed again and she left the trapeze again, going up and up and up, almost to the top of the tent until she described the wonderful series of backward somersaults that brought her down again to the trapeze. She was tiny way up there and then she grew as she came down. She stepped off the trapeze and came sliding down a rope. She bowed to the elephants. She bowed to everybody. She came over to him. He told her she was wonderful on the trapeze. She said it was really not at all difficult and anyone could do it. He could do it. He said he couldn't do it. He told her he was afraid. She laughed and told him he was silly to be afraid. She took his arm and led him toward the rope. The bright orange satin was flesh of flame on her thin body. She opened her mouth to laugh at him and he saw many gold inlays among her teeth. He pleaded with her to take him away from this high, dizzy place, this swirling peril. The trapeze came up to the limit of its whizzing arc and she left the trapeze, took him with her and they went up, somersaulting backward together, going up and over and he fought to get away from her and she laughed at him and he fought and fought until he got away from her. He went down alone. Down fast, face foremost, watching the sawdust and the faces and the colossal dull green elephants coming toward him. Down there they were attempting to do something for him. They were trying to arrange a net to catch him. Before they could get the net connected he was in amongst them, plunging past them and landing on his face. He felt the impact hammering into his face, the pain tearing through his face, hitting the back of his head and bouncing back and running all over his face. He was flat on his back, his arms wide, his legs spread wide as he looked up at the faces looking down on him. The pain was fierce and he moaned and the mob stood there and pitied him. He could see her high up there. The orange satin twirled and glimmered as she went away from the trapeze in another backward somersault. She came down wonderfully on the trapeze and although she was way up there her face was very close to his eyes and she was laughing at him and the gold inlays were dazzling in her laughing mouth.

The pain was fierce. It was a burning pain and there was something above the pain that felt very heavy on his face. He opened his eyes. He looked up at Coley.

"All over," Coley said.

The taxi driver was standing beside Coley working on a new cigar.

Coley had his arms folded and he looked down at Parry and said, "Stay there for a while. Don't try to talk. Don't move your mouth. I've got you all taped up. I've left a small space in front of your mouth so you'll be able to take nourishment. You'll use a glass straw and you can have anything liquid. If you want to smoke you can use a cigarette holder. But I don't want you to move your mouth and I don't want you to try talking. The bandages can come off after five days. When the bandages come off you'll look in the mirror and you'll see a new face. It'll be all healed by then and you can shave."

Parry's eyes talked to Coley.

Coley said, "There won't be any scars. I did a sensational job on you. I think it's the best job I've ever done. And I've done a lot of exciting things to people's faces. I've got it down pat, hiding those scars."

The pain was digging and tugging and digging. It was burning there in Parry's face and gradually he began to feel it in his arms. He looked at Coley. His eyes asked another question.

Coley answered, "I took off your coat and rolled up your shirtsleeves. I worked on your arms. The upper part of the underarm. Up near the armpit, where you can spare the flesh. I used that flesh on your face. Now I'm going to ask you a question and if the answer is yes I want you to nod very slowly. Do you have a place to stay?"

Parry nodded slowly.

"Do you have someone to help you?"

Parry nodded again.

"All right," Coley said. "When you get there you can talk to that person with paper and pencil. Now here's the ticket. You're to sleep flat on your back. Have this person tie your hands to something so you won't be able to turn over. During the day I want you to take it easy. Sit in one place most of the time and read or listen to the radio or play solitaire. Keep your mind off your face and above all keep your hands away from your face. In another day or so it's going to start itching but no matter how bad it is I want you to keep your hands off those bandages. I guess you can get up now."

Parry sat up. He took himself off the chair. His shirt was open a few buttons down from the collar and his sleeves were rolled up high. The upper parts of his arms were bandaged. He looked at his arms, he looked at Coley and Coley nodded. Parry rolled his sleeves down and buttoned them. He buttoned up his shirt and put on his necktie and got into his coat. Then he walked over to the mirror and took a look at himself.

He saw his eyes and his nose and a small hole in front of his mouth. He saw most of his forehead and his ears and his hair. The rest was all white bandage, the white gauze padded thickly on his face, the criss-cross of adhesive going back along with the bandage around the back of his head. The bandage went under his chin and around his jaws and slanted down around his neck.

Coley came over and stood beside him. He said, "There's a lot of wax and goo under that bandage. It's hard now but in a couple of days it'll be soft and part of it will become part of your new face."

Parry glanced at his wrist watch. It said 4:31. He looked at Coley.

Coley said, "Ninety minutes. Just like I told you."

The taxi driver said, "We better get moving."

Parry was looking at Coley and holding out his hand. Coley took the hand. Coley said, "Maybe you did it and maybe you didn't. I don't know. Sam claims you didn't do it and I've known Sam a long time. I have a lot of faith in his ideas about things. That's the main reason I took this job. If I thought you were a professional killer I wouldn't have any part of it. But the way it is now I've given you a new face and you've given me two hundred dollars and that's as far as it goes. I never keep records of my patients and I never make an effort to remember names. When you walk out of here you're through with me and I'm through with you."

Parry looked at the taxi driver. The taxi driver walked to the door, opened it, went to the other door, opened it and stood there looking up and down the hall. Then he turned and beckoned to Parry, and Parry went out there with him and they went down the hall and down the stairs. They were out in the alley and down a second alley that led to a small side street. The taxi was parked there. They got in and the two doors closed and the motor started.

The taxi driver used side streets, used them deftly, making good time without too much speed. Parry leaned back and closed his eyes. He was very tired. He was very thankful he had a place to go to and a friend to help him. The pain kept digging into his face and banging away at his arms but now he didn't mind. He had a place to stay. He had Fellsinger. He had a new face. Now he really had something that amounted to a chance.

The taxi came to a stop.

Parry looked out the window. They were home.

The taxi driver turned and looked at him and said, "How is it?"

Parry nodded.

"Think you can make it alone?"

Parry nodded again. He took bills from his pocket, picked out a fifty dollar bill and handed it to the driver. The driver looked at the bill and then offered it back. Parry shook his head.

The taxi driver said, "I'm not doing this on a cash basis."

Parry nodded. The taxi driver made another attempt to return the bill. Parry shook his head.

The taxi driver said, "Now you're sure you can make it?"

Parry nodded. He started to open the door. The taxi driver touched his wrist. He said, "You don't know me. I don't know you. You'll never see me again. I'll never see you again. You don't know the name of the men who fixed your face. Or put it this way. You always had the face you have now. You were never in a courtroom. You were never in San Quentin. You were never married. And you don't know me and I don't know you. How does that sound?"

Parry nodded.

The taxi driver said, "Thanks for the tip, mister."

Parry stepped out of the taxi. The taxi went into first gear and went on down the street. Parry walked up to the door of the apartment house, went in, and from his coat pocket he took the key that Fellsinger had given him. He opened the inner door.

In the elevator he wondered if Fellsinger had a cigarette holder up there. He was in great need of a cigarette. The elevator climbed four floors and came to a stop. Parry walked down the hall. He wondered if Fellsinger had a glass straw in there. He wondered how it would be to take rum through a glass straw. He wished Fellsinger had some gin around. He wanted gin and he wanted a cigarette. He had a feeling that falling asleep tonight would be hard work. He was at the door of Fellsinger's apartment and he put the key in the door and turned it and opened the door and went in.

It was dark in there, but light from the hall showed Parry the switch on the wall near the door. He flicked the switch and closed the door, facing the door as he closed it and then turning slowly and facing the room. He looked at Fellsinger.

Fellsinger was on the floor with his head caved in.

CHAPTER 11

There was blood all over Fellsinger, blood all over the floor. There were pools of it and ribbons of it. There were blotches of it, big blotches of it near Fellsinger, smaller blotches getting even smaller in progression away from the body. There were flecks of it on the furniture and suggestions of it on a wall. There was the cardinal luster of it and the smell of it and the feeling of it coming up from Fellsinger's busted skull and dancing around and settling down wherever it pleased. It was dark blood where it clotted in the skull cavities. It was luminous pale blood where it stained the horn of the trumpet that rested beside the body. The horn of the trumpet was slightly dented. The pearl buttons of the trumpet valves were pink from the spray of blood.

Fellsinger was belly down on the floor, but his face was twisted sideways. His eyes were opened wide, the pupils up high with a lot of white underneath. It was as if he was trying to look back. Either he wanted to see how badly he was hurt or he wanted to see who was banging on his skull with the trumpet. His mouth was halfway open and the tip of his tongue flapped over the side of his mouth.

Without sound, Parry said, "Hello, George."

Without sound, Fellsinger said, "Hello, Vince."

"Are you dead, George?"

"Yes, I'm dead."

"Why are you dead, George?"

"I can't tell you, Vince. I wish I could tell you but I can't."

"Who did it, George?"

"I can't tell you, Vince. Look at me. Look what happened to me. Isn't it awful?"

"George, I didn't do it. You know that."

"Of course, Vince. Of course you didn't do it."

"George, you don't really believe I did it."

"I know you didn't do it."

"I wasn't here, George. I couldn't have done it. Why would I want to kill you, George? You were my friend."

"Yes, Vince. I was your friend."

"George, you were my best friend. You were always a real friend."

"You were my only friend, Vince. My only friend."

"I know that, George. And I know I didn't kill you. I know it I know it I know it I know it I know it."

"Don't carry on like that, Vince."

"George, you're not really dead, are you?"

"Yes, Vince. I'm dead. And it's real, Vince, it's real. I'm really dead. I never thought I'd be important. But now I'm very important. They'll have me in all the papers."

"They'll say I killed you."

"Yes, Vince. That's what they'll say."

"But I didn't do it, George."

"I know, Vince. I know you didn't do it. I know who did it but I can't tell you because I'm dead."

"George, can I do anything for you?"

"No. You can't do a thing for me. I'm dead. Your friend George Fellsinger is dead."

"George, who do you think did it?"

"I tell you I know who did it. But I can't say."

"Give me a hint. Give me an idea."

"Vince, I can't give you anything. I'm dead."

"Maybe if I look around I'll find something."

"Don't do that, Vince. Don't move from where you are now. If you step in the blood you're going to make footprints."

"Footprints won't make any difference one way or another. As soon as they find you here they'll say I did it."

"Yes, Vince. That's what they'll say. You can't do anything about that. But if you give them footprints you'll be throwing everything away. What I mean is, if they have the footprints they'll have more than a conclusion. They'll have you, because they have means of tracing footprints, tracing right through to the store where the shoes were bought. When they get that they'll get her. And if they get her they'll get you, because you can't operate without her."

"George, I can't go back to her."

"What do you mean, you can't go back? You've got to go back. You can't go anyplace else. Where else could you go?"

"I don't know, George. I don't know. But I can't go back to her."

"Jesus Christ."

"I can't help it, George. I can't go back to her. I can't bring her back into it now."

"But she wants to help you, Vince."

"Why, George? How do you make it out? Why does she want to help me?"

"She feels sorry for you."

"There's more to it than that. There's much more. What is it?"

"I don't know, Vince."

"I can't go back to her."

"You've got to go back. You've got to stay there for five days. You need someone to take care of you until those

110

bandages come off. Then when you go away you can really go away. You'll have a new face. You'll have a new life. You always talked about travel. Places you wanted to see. I remember the things you said. How grand it would be to get away. From everybody. From everything. How I felt bad about it when you said that, because I figured our friendship was one of those very valuable things that don't happen very often between plain guys like you and me. How I hoped you'd include me in your plans to go away. You knew that. You knew how I felt. And I had an idea that when you finally went away you would take me with you. To that beach town in Spain. Or that place in Peru. Was it Patavilca."

"Yes, George. It was Patavilca?"

"Patavilca in Peru. Jumping out of our cages in an investment security house. Jumping out of our cages in dried-up apartment houses. Going away, going away from it, all of it, going to Patavilca, in Peru. With nothing to do down there except get the sun and sleep on the beach. They showed that beach in the travel folder. It was a lovely beach. And they showed us the streets and the houses. The little streets and the little houses under the sun. I was waiting for you to say the word. I was waiting for you to say let's pack up and go."

"Why didn't you say the word, George? Why didn't you take the bull by the horns? There wouldn't have been any trial. This trouble would have never happened."

"You know why I didn't say the word. You know me. Guys like me come a dime a dozen. No fire. No backbone. Dead weight waiting to be pulled around and taken to places where we want to go but can't go alone. Because we're afraid to go alone. Because we're afraid to be alone. Because we can't face people and we can't talk to people. Because we don't know how. Because we can't handle life and don't know the first thing about taking a bite out of life. Because we're afraid and we don't know what we're afraid of and still we're afraid. Guys like me."

"You had ideas, George."

"I had ideas that I thought were great. But I was always afraid to let them loose. Once you were up here and I put my entire attitude toward life into a trumpet riff. You told me it was cosmic-ray stuff. Something from a billion miles away, bouncing off the moon, coming down and into my brain and coming out of my trumpet. You told me I should do something with ideas like that. And I agreed with you but I never did anything because I was afraid. And now I'm dead."

"I think I better be going now."

"Yes, Vince. You go now. You go to her."

"George, I'm afraid."

"You go to her. Stay there five days. Then go to Patavilca, in Peru. Stay there the rest of your life."

"I can't see myself going away."

"You've got to see that. You've got to do that. You've got to go far away and stay there."

"I wish I knew who killed you."

"It doesn't make any difference. I'm dead now."

"And that's why it makes a difference. Because you're dead. And they'll say I killed you, just as they said I killed her. And I said I didn't kill her. I said it was an accident. All along I said it was an accident and that's what I believed. I always believed she fell down and hit her head on that ash tray. I don't believe that any more. I know someone killed her and that same someone killed you."

"You're curious, Vince. And you're getting angry. That won't do. You can't be curious and you can't be angry. You've got to think in terms of getting away, and only that. And now you better go."

"Good-by, George."

Parry switched off the light. He stepped out of the apartment and closed the door slowly. There was a stiff-

112

ness in his legs as he walked down the corridor. In the elevator he had a feeling he was going to faint. He sagged against the wall of the elevator and he was going to the floor and as his knees gave way he put his hands on the wall and braced himself and made himself stay up.

On the street he tried to walk fast but his legs were very stiff and he couldn't get any go into them. The pain in his face mixed with the pain in his arms and he wanted to get down on the pavement and sleep. He kept walking. He looked at his wrist watch and it said a few minutes past five and he looked up and saw the beginnings of morning sifting through the black sieve. He walked down the empty quiet streets.

He walked a mile and knew he had another mile to go. He didn't think he could make it. A taxi came down the street and he turned and saw the driver looking at him. He was tempted to take the taxi. But he knew he couldn't take a taxi. Not now. Not at this stage. The taxi slowed down and the driver was waiting for him to make a move. He kept walking. He faced straight ahead, knowing that the taxi driver was regarding his bandaged head with increasing curiosity. He kept walking. The taxi picked up speed and went down the street and made a turn.

A glow came onto the pavement, dripping from the grey light getting through the black sky. Parry walked past a cheap hotel and stopped and looked back at the sign. He was tempted to go in and take a room. He was so tired. The pain was so bad. He was so very, very tired.

He kept walking. Now he was going faster and he knew he was racing the morning. He knew he couldn't keep it up like this, and if he didn't get there soon he was going to go out cold. He knew he couldn't afford to go out cold and he kept walking fast. He was getting there. He was almost there. He measured the streets. He told himself it was three blocks. He knew it was more than three, more on the order of six or seven. He didn't think he could last out

113

seven blocks. They were long blocks. The morning was getting a lead on him. He tried to walk faster. He tried to run and his legs became cotton fluff under him and he went to the pavement. He stayed there on his knees, feeling a wetness flowing all over his body, and for a few moments he thought it was the blood from his face getting out through the split flesh and pouring down under the bandage and down through his collar and going all over him. He put his hand to the under-edge of the bandage. His hand came away moist. He looked at his hand. It glistened with perspiration. He stood up and started to walk. He asked the blocks to come toward him, slide toward him and go away behind him. He kept walking. Then he could see it, the apartment house. He started to open his mouth to let out a cry and a dreadful pain spread out from his lips and went to his eyes and came down to his lips again. He closed his mouth, and his eyes were jammed with tears. He looked at the apartment house coming toward him as he went toward it. He was about sixty steps away from the apartment house. He didn't think he could cover those sixty steps. He covered five of them and ten of them and thirty of them. He was ahead of the morning now and he was going to make it and he knew it. And as he knew that he knew it he saw something on the other side of the street, almost at the end of the block, parked there and waiting there and it was the Studebaker.

CHAPTER 12

It was the same Studebaker. It was the very same, the same Studebaker from way back. The same hunk of junk that had picked him up on the road. It couldn't be. It just couldn't be. And yet it was. There it was, parked across the street. There it was. Waiting there. The same Studebaker.

Parry came toward the apartment house, not knowing he was going toward the apartment house, knowing only that he was going toward the Studebaker, wanting to make sure that it was the same car and knowing it was the same car and not believing it was the same car and knowing it anyway. There was nobody in the car. It couldn't be the same car.

It was the same car.

He didn't want to start asking himself why. And how. And why and how and when and how and why and how and why. He asked and he couldn't answer. If there was any answer at all it was coincidence. But there was a limit to coincidence and this was way past the limit. This neighborhood aimed toward upper middle class, anywhere from fifteen thousand a year on up. Or give Studebaker a break and make it ten thousand. Even seventy-five hundred and

115

still Studebaker didn't belong around here. Studebaker was way down in the sharecropper category. And the car was parked in front of an apartment house that wouldn't rent closet space for less than one ten a month. It couldn't be the same car.

It was the same car.

All right, Studebaker worked there as a janitor. No. All right, Studebaker had a wealthy brother living there. No. All right, Studebaker was driving down the street and he ran out of gas and had to park there. No. No and no and no.

It wasn't the same car. It couldn't be the same car.

It was the same car.

The morning light came down and tried to glimmer on the Studebaker. There was no polish on the Studebaker and very little paint, therefore very little glimmer. There was only the old Studebaker coupé, dull and quiet there on the other side of the street, waiting for him.

Parry turned and went toward the apartment house. He was staggering now. On the steps he stumbled and fell. In the vestibule his finger went toward the wrong button and he veered it away just in time and got it going toward the right button and pressed the button.

He got a buzz. He went through the lobby and entered the elevator. He pressed the 3 button. The elevator started up and Parry felt himself going down. As the elevator went up he kept going down and his eyes were closed now. He saw the black wall of his shut eyelids and then he saw the bright orange and the trapeze again and he saw the gold inlays in the laughing mouth and then he saw the black again just before everything became bright orange and after that it was all black and he was going in there in the black and he was in there. He was in the black.

Gradually the black gave way and its place was taken by grey-violet and yellow. He was on the sofa. He looked up

116

and he saw her. She was standing beside the sofa, watching him. She smiled.

She said, "I didn't think you'd come back."

She was wearing a yellow robe. Her yellow hair came down and sprayed her shoulders.

She said, "When I heard the buzzer I was frightened. When nobody came up I was terribly frightened. Then after a while I went out in the hall and I saw the light from the elevator. I went down there and I opened the elevator and I saw you in there. I was so very frightened when I saw the bandages but I recognized the suit and so I understood the bandages. I'm lucky you're not heavy, because otherwise I couldn't have managed it. Tell me what happened to you."

Parry shook his head.

"Why not?"

He shook his head.

"Why can't you tell me?"

He pointed to his mouth. He shook his head.

"Can you talk?"

He shook his head.

"Can I do anything for you?"

He shook his head. Then he nodded. With an imaginary pencil he scribbled on a palm. She hurried out of the room. She came back with a pad and a pencil.

Parry wrote—

A taxi driver recognized me. He offered to help me. He took me to a plastic specialist who operated on my face. Then he brought me back and left me off a few blocks from here. The bandages must stay on for five days. I can eat only liquids and I've got to take them through a glass straw. I can smoke cigarettes if you have a holder. I've got to sleep on my back and to keep from turning over on my face I've

117

got to have my wrists tied to the sides of the bed. My face hurts terribly and so do my arms where he had to cut to get new skin for my face. I'm very tired and I want to sleep.

She read what he had written. She said, "You'll sleep in the bedroom. I'll sleep here on the sofa."

He shook his head.

"I said you'll sleep in the bedroom. Please don't argue with me. I'm your nurse now. You mustn't argue with the nurse."

She led him into the bedroom. She stayed out while he undressed. When he was under the covers he knocked on the side of the bed and she came in. She used handkerchiefs to tie his wrists to the sides of the bed.

"Is that too tight?"

He shook his head.

"Are you comfortable?"

He nodded.

"Anything more I can do?"

He shook his head.

"Good night, Vincent."

She switched off the light and went out of the room.

In a few minutes Parry was asleep. He was up a few times during the night, coming out of sleep when he tried to turn over and his tied wrists held him back. Aside from that he slept the full sleep of fatigue, the heavy sleep that got him away from shock and pain. He slept until late in the afternoon, and when he awoke she was in the room, waiting for him with a breakfast tray. There was a tall glass of orange juice. There was a bowl of white cereal, very soft and mostly cream, so that it could be taken through a glass straw. There was a pot of coffee and a glass of water. There were three glass straws, new and glinting, and he knew she had gone out in the morning to buy them. He thanked her with his eyes. She smiled at him. She reached for something on the bureau and when she held it up he saw a long cigarette holder, new and glinting. It was yellow enamel and it had a small, delicately shaped mouthpiece.

She said, "Did you sleep well?"

He nodded. She untied the handkerchiefs and he started to get out of the bed and then he looked at her. She walked out of the room. He went into the bathroom. When he was finished in the bathroom he took his breakfast through the glass straws. Basie music came from the phonograph in the other room, then she came in from the other room and lighted a cigarette and watched him sip his meal through the straws. She looked at the empty glasses, the empty bowl and the empty cup.

She smiled and said, "That's a good boy. And now would you like a cigarette?"

He nodded.

She placed a cigarette in the holder and lighted it for him.

She said, "Does your face feel better today?"

He nodded.

"Much better?"

He nodded.

"What would you like to do?"

He shrugged.

"Would you like to read?"

He nodded.

"What would you like to read?"

He shrugged.

"A magazine?"

He shook his head.

"The paper?"

He looked at her. She wasn't smiling. He tried to get something from her eyes. He couldn't get anything. He started a nod and then he stopped it and he shrugged.

119

She went out of the room and came back with an afternoon edition. She gave it to him and he held it close to his eyes and saw that in San Francisco a man named Fellsinger had been murdered in the early hours of the morning and police said it was the work of the escaped lifer from San Quentin. Police said Parry's fingerprints were all over the place, on the furniture, on the cellophane wrapping around a pack of cigarettes, on a glass, on practically everything except the murder weapon, which was a trumpet. Police put it this way—they said Vincent Parry had gone to his friend George Fellsinger and had demanded aid in his effort to get away. Fellsinger no doubt refused. Then Fellsinger tried to call the police or told Parry he would eventually call the police. In rage or calm decision Parry took hold of the trumpet forgetting his other fingerprints throughout the room and knowing only that he mustn't get his fingerprints on the trumpet. And so he must have used a handkerchief around his hand as he wielded the trumpet and brought it down on Fellsinger's head. Again and again and again. The only fingerprints in the place were those of Fellsinger and those of Parry. There was positively no doubt about it. Parry did it.

Parry looked up. She was watching him. He pointed to the story.

She nodded. She said, "Yes, Vincent. I saw it."

He made a gesture to indicate that she should offer a further reaction.

She said, "I don't know what to say. Did you do it?"

He shook his head.

"But who could have done it?"

He shook his head.

"You were there last night?"

He nodded. Then he made the pad and pencil gesture. She brought him the pad and the pencil and he wrote it out for her, as it had happened. She read it slowly. It was as if she was studying from a textbook.

When she finally put the pad down she said, "In that statement you wrote this morning you said nothing about Fellsinger. Why?"

He shrugged.

"Is there anything else you didn't tell me?"

He shook his head. He thought of the Studebaker. He thought of Max. And the Studebaker. And he shook his head again.

She said, "I know there's something else. I wish you'd tell me. The more you tell me the more help I can give you. But I can't force you to tell me. I only ask if it's important."

He shook his head.

She went to the door and there she turned and faced him. She said, "I have work to do this afternoon. Settlement work. I devote a few hours every day to it. I'll be back at six and we'll have dinner. Promise me you'll stay here. Promise me you won't answer the buzzer and no matter what takes place and no matter what thoughts get into your head you'll stay here."

He nodded.

She said, "There are cigarettes in the other room and if you get thirsty you'll find oranges in the refrigerator and you can make juice."

He nodded.

She walked out. He leaned over the newspaper and a few times more he read the Fellsinger story. He heard her going out of the apartment. He went through the newspaper. He tried to get interested in the financial section and gradually he succeeded and he was going through the stock quotations, the Dow-Jones averages, the prices on wheat and cotton, the situation in railroads and steel. He saw a small and severely neat advertisement from the firm where he had worked as a clerk, where Fellsinger had worked. He began to remember the days of work, the day he had started there, how difficult it was at first, how hard he had tried, how he had taken a correspondence course in statistics shortly after his marriage, hoping he could get a grasp on statistics and ultimately step up to forty-five a week as a statistician. But the correspondence course gave him more questions than answers and finally he had to give it up. He remembered the night he wrote the letter telling them to stop sending the mimeographed sheets. He showed the letter to Gert and she told him he would never get anywhere. She went out that night. He remembered he hoped she would never come back and he was afraid she would never come back because there was something about her that got him at times and he wished there was something about him that got her. He knew there was nothing about him that got her and he wondered why she didn't pick herself up and walk out once and for all. She was always talking in terms of tall bony men with high cheekbones and hollow cheeks and very tall. He was bony and very thin and he had high cheekbones and hollow cheeks but he wasn't tall. He was really a miniature of what she really wanted. And because she couldn't get a permanent hold on the genuine she figured she might as well stay with the miniature. That was about as close as he could come to it. She was very thin herself and that was the way he liked them, thin. Very thin. She had practically no front development and nothing in back but that was the way he liked them and the first time he saw her he concentrated on the way she was constructed like a reed and he was interested. He disregarded the eyes that were more colorless than light brown, the hair that was more colorless than pale-brown flannel, the nose that was thin and the mouth that was very thin and the blade-line of her jaw. He disregarded the fact that she was twenty-nine when she married him and the only reason she married him was because he was a miniature of what she really wanted and she hadn't been able to get what she really wanted. She married him because he came along at a time when she was beginning to worry about it, to worry that she wouldn't be able to get anything. There were times when she told him the only reason he married her was because he was beginning to worry, because he couldn't get what he wanted and he supposed he might as well take this colorless reed while the taking was good, and before years caught up with him and he wouldn't be able to get anything at all. He said that wasn't true. He wanted to marry her because she was something he really wanted and if she would only work along with him they would be able to get along and they would find ways to be happy. He tried to make her happy. He thought a child would make her happy. He tried to give her a child and once he got one started but she went to a doctor and took pills. She said she hated the thought of having a child.

Parry turned the pages of the newspaper and came to the sports section. Basketball was scheduled for tonight. He remembered he had always liked basketball. He remembered he had played basketball while he was in the reformatory in Arizona, and later he had played on a Y.M.C.A. team when he was living alone in San Francisco and working in a stock room for sixteen a week. He remembered he went to the games every now and then and one week end he went up to Eugene in Oregon to see a great Oregon State team play a great Oregon team. He remembered how he wanted to see that game, and how happy he was when finally he was in there with the crowd and the teams were on the floor and the game was getting under way. He remembered once he took Gert to a game on a Saturday night and it was after they were married four months. She kept saying she wasn't interested in basketball and she would rather see a floor show somewhere. He kept saying she ought to give basketball a chance because it was really something exciting to see and after all it was a change from floor shows. She said it was because seats for the basketball game were only a buck and a half or somewhere around that and he just didn't want to put out nine or ten or eleven in a night club. He said that wasn't a fair thing to say, because he was always taking her wherever she wanted to go on Saturday night, and she always wanted to go to night clubs, and it wasn't nine or ten or eleven anyway, it was more on the order of sixteen and seventeen and nineteen, because they both did considerable drinking. He didn't say the other things he was thinking then, that when she was in the night clubs she kept looking at tall, bony men, always kept looking at them, never looking at him, never listening to him, always kept turning her head to look at tall, bony men with high cheekbones and hollow cheeks. How he would finally stop talking and she wouldn't even realize he had stopped talking. Yet that night she had finally condescended to go to the basketball game with him. And it was an exciting game, it was very close, getting hotter all the time, and he was all pepped up and he was happy to be here. She was sitting beside him, he remembered, not saying anything, not asking him about the game, not curious about the way it was played, but interested nonetheless. Interested in the tall bony boys who ran up and down the floor. Interested in their tall bony bodies, their long arms, their long legs glimmering in the bright light of the basketball court as they ran and stopped and ran again. And when she had seen all of them that she could see, she said she was fed up looking at all that nonsense down there, a bunch of young fools trying to cripple each other so they could throw a ball through a hoop. She said she wanted to leave. He asked her to stay with him until the game was over. She said she wanted to leave. She said if he didn't leave with her she would go alone. She was talking loud. He begged her to lower her voice. She talked louder. People around them were telling them to keep quiet and watch the game. She talked louder. Finally he said all right, they would leave. As they got up and started to leave he could hear other men laughing at him.

Parry turned the pages and arrived at the woman's section. Somebody was telling the women how to cook something. He remembered she hated to cook. They ate out most of the time. There were nights when he came home very tired and he cringed at the thought of going out and standing in line at the popular and expensive restaurants she liked, and how he wished she would learn to cook, because even on the few nights when they ate at home she gave him uncooked food, cold cuts or canned fish and the only thing hot was the coffee. Once he tried to talk to her about it and she started to yell. She took the percolator and poured the coffee all over the floor.

He remembered she took two thirds, more than two thirds of the thirty-five a week he made. He remembered she hardly ever smiled at him. When she did smile it wasn't really a smile, it was because she was amused at something. She never told him what amused her. And things that amused her didn't amuse him. He remembered once they were walking down the street and there was a traffic jam and one car bumped into another and they locked bumpers. She said, "Good." She started to laugh. He tried to see something funny in it. He tried to laugh. He couldn't laugh.

Once they were walking toward the apartment house and a delivery boy passed them on a bicycle, with the wire tray heaped with packages on the handle bars. The bicycle hit a bump and turned over. The boy fell on his face and the packages went flying all over the street. The boy had a cut on his face and he was sitting there in the street and putting a handkerchief to the blood on his face. She started to laugh. He asked her what she was laughing at. She didn't answer. She kept on laughing.

He was beginning to feel tired again. The pain in his face was dull now, and he was getting accustomed to it. But as he sat there measuring the pain he gradually realized there was something else besides the pain. Like little feathers under the bandage. That was the itch Coley had talked about. The healing process, the mending was under way. He welcomed the itch. He told it to get worse. He turned the pages of the newspaper and saw nothing to catch his interest, and besides he was very tired. He pushed the newspaper aside and let his head go back against the pillow. He closed his eyes, knowing he wouldn't sleep, knowing he would just stay there, resting. Feeling the pain, feeling the itch under the bandage, flowing into the pain, then crawling under the pain. Once he opened his eyes and looked toward the window. There was going to be rain in San Francisco. The sky was a heavy, muttering grey, getting ready to let loose. He closed his eyes again. He didn't care if it rained. He was here, he was in here, he was all right in here. And in less than five days he would be out of here and he would be going away with his new face and everything would be all right. And the buzzer was sounding and everything would be all right. And the buzzer was sounding.

He sat up.

The buzzer was sounding again. Then it stopped. He sat there waiting. It sounded again. It was a needle going into him. And then it stopped.

He waited. He wondered who it was down there. He took himself off the bed and walked to the window and waited there. Then he saw someone going away from the apartment house and walking across the street, walking toward the Studebaker that was parked on the other side of the street. And it was the man who had given him the lift. It was Studebaker.

It was really Studebaker, with different clothes, new clothes and no hat, and really Studebaker. And Studebaker was looking for him. Studebaker alone. No police. Parry couldn't get that, couldn't get anywhere near it.

The sky gave way. Rain came down.

Parry stood there at the window and watched Studebaker getting into the car. The car crawled, jolted, went forward, went on down to the corner and made a turn. Parry began to quiver. Studebaker was going to the police. But why now? Why not before? Why now? If Studebaker hadn't talked to the police until now, why was he going to see them now?

The rain came down hard and steadily. Parry went away from the window, went toward the bed, then stopped and went toward the dresser and stood before the dresser, looking in the mirror. He decided to take off the bandage and get out of the apartment before Studebaker came back with the police. He brought his hands to his face and his fingers came against the adhesive. He tugged at the adhesive. A tremendous burst of pain shot across his face and went leaping through his head. His fingers came away from the adhesive. He told himself that he mustn't be afraid of the pain. He must try again. He must get out of here, and he couldn't afford to be wearing the bandage when he went out. He got his fingers on the adhesive and once more he tugged at it and once more the pain slashed away at him. He knew he wouldn't be able to stand any more of it. He decided to stay here and let them come and get him. He went into the living room and seated himself on the sofa and looked at the floor. He sat there for a while, and then he got up and went into the bedroom and got the cigarette holder. He returned to the living room and picked up a pack of cigarettes.

He sat there looking at the floor and smoking cigarettes. He smoked nine cigarettes in succession. He looked at the stubs in the ash tray. He counted them, saw them dead there in the heaped ashes. Then he wondered how long it would take until the police arrived. He wondered how long it would be until he was dead, because this time he wouldn't be going back to a cell. This time they had him on a charge that would mean the death sentence. He looked at the window and saw the thick rain coming out of the thick grey sky, the broken sky. He decided to take a run at the window and go through the glass and finish the whole thing. He took a step toward the window and then stopped and turned his back to the window and looked at the wall. He stood there without moving for almost a full hour. He was going back and taking chunks out of his life and holding them up to examine them. The young and bright yellow days in the hot sun of Maricopa, always bright yellow in every season. The wide and white roads going north from Arizona. The grey and violet of San Francisco. The grey and the heat of the stock room, and the days and nights of nothing, the years of nothing. And the cage in the investment security house, and the stiff white collars of the executives, stiff and newly white every day, and their faces every day, and their voices every day. And the paper, the plain white paper, the pink paper, the pale-green paper, the paper ruled violet and green and black in small ledgers and larger ledgers and immense ledgers. And the faces. The faces of statisticians who made forty-five a week, and customers' men who sometimes made a hundred and a half and sometimes made nothing. And the executives who made fifteen and twenty and thirty thousand a year, and the customers who sat there or stood there and watched the board. The customers, and some of them could walk out of that place and get on their yachts and go out across thousands of miles of water, getting up in the morning when they felt like getting up, fishing or swimming around their grand white yachts, alone out there on the water. And in the evening they would be wearing emerald studs in their shirt-fronts with white formal jackets and black tropical worsted trousers with satin black and gleaming down the sides, down to their gleaming black patent-leather shoes as they danced in the small ballrooms of their yachts with tall thin women with bared shoulders, dripping organdie from their tall thin bodies as they danced or held delicate glasses of champagne in their thin, delicate fingers. And when these customers came back to the investment security house they came in their gleaming black limousines and they came in very much tanned and smiling and he would be there in his cage, looking at them, thinking it was a pity such fortunate people had to eventually die, because it was really worthwhile for them to live on and on, they had so much to live for, they had so many things to enjoy. He liked to see them coming in wearing their expensive clothes, smoking their expensive cigars, talking with their expensive voices. He was so very glad when they came in, when they stood where he could see them, because he got a lift just looking at them. There were times when he wished he could talk to them, when he wished he had the nerve to start a conversation with one of them. If he could only have a talk with one of them so he could hear all about the wonderful things, the wonderful houses they lived in, the wonderful trips they made, the wonderful wonderful things they did. As he looked at them, as he thought of the lives they led, the luxuries they enjoyed, he decided that if he used his head and had some luck he might be able to climb up toward where they were. That was all it really was, a matter of using his head and having a little luck, and he decided to get started. And that was about the time when he decided to take the correspondence course in statistics.

He went into the living room and put another cigarette in the holder. He put himself on the sofa and rested there, sucking at the holder. He tried to build a mental microscope to deal with these tiny things he had on the table of his mind. He came to a point that became a wall and he couldn't slide under or climb over. He had to stay there. Now he was getting tired again. He took the stub out of the holder, crushed it in a tray. He let his head go back against the softness of the sofa. His eyes closed and the thoughts circled his brain, circled more slowly, and slowly, and then he was asleep.

The door opening pulled him away from sleep. He sat up and looked at her. She was closing the door. Her arms were heaped with packages. Now she came toward him. She said, "How do you feel?"

He nodded.

"Everything all right?"

He nodded.

She said, "Punctual, am I not? It's exactly six. And now we'll have some dinner. Feel hungry?"

He nodded.

She went into the kitchen. He could hear her moving around in there. He waited on the sofa, waited for dinner, waited for the buzzer to sound again, waited for Studebaker to come up with the police.

The dinner tasted fine, even though it went in through the glass straw. There was beef broth, there was the tan cream of a vegetable-beef stew, there was a butterscotch pudding thinned down to liquid. He gestured his willingness to help with the dishes. She told him to go into the other room and play some records. He went in and got a Basie going under the needle. It was *Sent For You Yesterday And Here You Come Today*. And Rushing was beginning to yell his heart out when the telephone rang.

Parry stood up. He looked at the telephone. It rang again just as Rushing repeated his cry that the moon looked lonely. She came out of the kitchen, looked at the phone, looked at Parry. She took a step toward the phone. It rang again. Parry lifted the needle from the record.

She looked at Parry as the phone rang again. She said, "There's nothing to worry about. I know who it is."

She picked up the phone.

"Hello? Oh, yes, hello, yes—yes?—oh, I've just had dinner—no, thanks anyway—well—well—all right, when can I expect you?—all right—right."

She put down the phone and looked at Parry. She said, "That was Bob Rapf. He'll be here in an hour."

CHAPTER 13

Parry raised his arms to indicate that he did not understand.

She said, "It'll be all right. You stay in the bedroom. He won't know you're here."

Parry gestured toward the bedroom, then raised his arms again.

She said, "He won't look in the bedroom."

Parry lowered his head and shook it slowly.

"Please don't worry about it," she said. He looked up. She was smiling at him.

He shrugged.

She went back in the kitchen. When she was finished with the dishes she came in and straightened the living room. As she emptied an ash tray she said, "I know you think it's a mistake, letting him come here. But it can't be any other way. I've known him for so long, I've been seeing so much of him lately, it's got to a point where I have a definite hold on him. I wish it wasn't that way. But as long as it is that way, I've got to go along with it. I know what happens to him when I refuse to see him. I wish I knew some way to break it without ripping him apart. But there doesn't seem to be any way to break it. All I can do is wait for it to die out."

She emptied another ash tray. She looked at him and saw that he was looking at her.

She said, "It's not physical. It never was. It never will be. It can't be. What he likes about me is the things I say, and the things he thinks I think about, the feelings he thinks I have. All he wants to do is be with me and talk to me and look at me and get a picture of the things I'm thinking. Even when I have nothing to say he just likes to be there with me. I don't know why I started it. I guess perhaps I started it because I felt sorry for him. He had no one to really be with."

All the ash trays were now emptied into one big tray. She took the tray into the kitchen. When she came out, she said, "I guess that's what it was. I was sorry for him. I still feel sorry for him. But I can't let it go on much further. Have you ever seen him?"

Parry shook his head.

"He's a good-looking man," she said. "He's thirty-nine now but he looks older. You can't see the grey in his hair because he's blond, but you can see the lines in his face. He has mild blue eyes, and that's the way all of him is, very mild, even though he's built heavy. And he's not very tall. He's a draftsman and he works at a shipyard. He likes expensive clothes. He likes to spend money. He and Madge had a baby but it died when it was less than a year old. Did she ever tell you about that?"

He nodded.

"Did she ever tell you about him?"

He nodded.

"I imagine she must have painted him badly. She did that when she spoke to me about him. That was after she knew I was seeing him. She didn't try to block it. She just struck up a close friendship with me, much closer than I liked, and she began to tell me things about him. She wasn't very clever about it, for instance she said he was cheap and of course she should have known that I knew differently. She said he was selfish and he isn't that way at all. What she wanted me to do was give him walking papers, not because she wanted him back, but because she wanted him to lose me. She still wants that. She wants him to lose everything. She keeps telling me I'd be doing myself a big favor if I closed the door on him."

Parry nodded.

"You mean you agree with her?"

He shook his head.

"Oh, you mean she told you the same thing. I suppose she tells everyone that. I can't understand her. She ought to realize she'll never be happy as long as she keeps interfering with him. Or maybe that's the only thing that gives her happiness. Interfering."

The buzzer sounded.

She frowned. "That can't be Bob. Much too early."

Parry stood up. It had to be Studebaker. And the police.

She said, "Go in the bedroom. I'll find out who it is."

Parry went into the bedroom and closed the door. He sat on the edge of the bed and he was hitting the joints of his fingers together. The itching under the bandage was beginning to grow, to spread, and he wanted to get at it. He sat there, hitting the joints of his fingers together. He heard a door opening. He heard voices and they were both feminine, and one of them belonged to Madge Rapf.

"But that's ridiculous," Irene was saying.

"Honey, honey, you've got to help me. I'm scared out of my wits," Madge said.

"Ridiculous."

"Why is it ridiculous?" Madge said. "Look what he did to George Fellsinger. You surely read about it. Why, he went up there and—it gives me the shakes just to think of it. And if he did that to George he'll do it to me. He's got it in for me, you know that. You're got to let me stay here,

134

honey. Let me hide here. Oh, let, let me—"

"Want a drink?"

"Yes, please honey, let me have a drink. Oh, my God, I'm in terrible shape. I haven't been able to eat a thing all day."

"Can I fix you something?" Irene said.

"No, I'm not hungry. How can I be hungry? He's going to kill me. He's going to look me up and when he finds me he'll—oh, God Almighty, what am I going to do?"

"Pull yourself together," Irene said. "They'll catch him."

"They haven't caught him yet. Listen, honey, as long as they haven't caught him I've got to hide. It was my testimony that sent him up. I tell you I'm so scared I don't know whether I'm coming or going."

"Sit down, Madge. Sit down and relax. You can't let yourself go to pieces like this."

Parry heard a series of dragging, grinding sobs.

Between the sobs, Madge was saying, "Let me stay here."

"I can't."

"Why not?"

"Well, I—I fail to see the necessity of it."

"Oh, I see. You don't want to be put out."

"It isn't that, Madge. Really, it isn't."

"Well, what is it, then? This place is big enough to hold two. It's—"

"It's this—I'm expecting Bob here any minute."

"All right, I'll hide. I'll go in the bedroom."

"No," Irene said. "Don't do that."

"Why not?"

"Well, it's—it's sort of cheap. You have nothing to hide. You have nothing to be ashamed of."

"That's one way of looking at it," Madge said. "And then of course there's another way." Now she sounded as if she was talking between puffs at a cigarette. "Of course, there's a chance he'd walk into the bedroom."

"Do you think he does that?"

"I don't know."

"If you don't know, why do you insinuate? I think we ought to understand each other, Madge. You can't make statements like that and expect me to take it without a whimper. You've said things on that order before, little needles here and there and every now and then, and I tried to think you didn't mean anything by it. But this time the needle's gone in just a bit deeper. And I don't like it. I want you to know I don't like it."

"Honey, you needn't get all excited. It wouldn't make any difference to me even if—"

"Please, Madge."

"Let me stay here, honey. I tell you I'm afraid to go out of here alone."

"This is silly."

"All right, it's silly, but that's the way it is with me and what can I do about it? For God's sake, honey, try to understand what a fix I'm in. You've got to let me stay here or else you've got to stay with me wherever I go. Oh, come on, honey, let's pack up—"

The buzzer sounded.

"You better go now, Madge."

"For God's sake—"

"Look, Madge. You go down the hall. Wait there until you hear the door closing. Then leave."

The buzzer sounded.

"But I'm afraid—"

"Madge, I don't want you to be here when he comes in."

"Why not?"

"Let's not start that again."

The buzzer sounded.

Parry stood up and looked at the window. He wondered if the window offered a way of reaching the fire escape. He knew it was Studebaker down there. It wasn't Bob Rapf. It was Studebaker. And the police.

"Go on, Madge. Go now."

"Oh, I'm so afraid."

"Go now, Madge."

The buzzer sounded.

"I won't go. I won't go out alone. I can't. Parry will find me. I know he'll find me. Oh, God, I'm so terribly afraid. Please, Irene—oh, honey, why won't you help me?"

The buzzer sounded and kept sounding.

"Look, Madge—"

"No, I won't go. No—I won't leave here alone." Madge was sobbing again, the grinding dragging sobs that dragged along with the buzzer as it kept sounding.

"All right, Madge. I'm going to let him come up."

The buzzer stopped sounding.

Parry walked toward the window, walked softly, slowly, came to the window and looked through the wet glass, wet on the other side where the rain was hitting. The rain was rapid and thick, racing down from the broken sky, dark grey now and mottled dark yellow and fading blue. Parry put his fingers on the window handles and started to bring pressure. The window wouldn't give. He stepped away from the window and watched the rain running down, oblique toward him, coming against the glass and washing down.

He heard the door opening.

He heard a man saying, "For Christ's sake—"

He heard Madge saying, "Hello, Bob."

He heard the man saying, "What takes place here?"

"Raining hard, Bob?" It was Irene.

"Pouring," Bob said. "But what I want to know is what takes place."

"Nothing very special," Irene said.

"I don't go for these deals," Bob said. "This looks as if it's been arranged."

"Why should anything be arranged?" Irene said.

"I don't know," Bob said. "For Christ's sake, Madge,

what's wrong with you?"

"I'm scared," Madge said. "Honey, should I tell him?"

"Tell me what?" Bob had a mild voice, trying to get away from mildness.

"Sure," Irene said. "Go on and tell him."

Madge said, "It's Vincent Parry. I'm scared he'll find me. He'll kill me."

"If he does," Bob said, "I'll look him up and shake his hand."

Madge let out a howl.

"Bob, that wasn't necessary," Irene said.

"I can't stand it," Madge sobbed. "I can't stand it any more."

"Neither can I," Bob said. "Why won't you leave people alone? Why do you go around finding excuses to come up here. Irene doesn't want you here. Nobody wants you. Because you're a pest. You're not satisfied unless you're bothering people. You got on your family's nerves, you got on my nerves, you get on everybody's nerves. Why don't you wise up already."

"Do you know what you are?" Madge said. "You're a hound. You have no feeling."

"No feeling for you," Bob said. "No feeling at all, except I'm annoyed whenever I see you."

"You married me," Madge said. "You're still married to me. Don't forget that."

"How can I forget it?" Bob said. "You see these lines on my face? They're anniversary presents. Irene, will you do me a favor? Will you ask her to please leave?"

"I won't go out of here alone," Madge said.

"She thinks Parry's looking for her. That's all he's got to do, look for her. Listen, Madge, if there's anyone Parry wants to avoid more than the police, it's you." Bob's voice was getting louder. "You're the last person he wants to kill. You're the last person he wants to see. And you know why. And you know I know why."

"What kind of a riddle is this?" Irene said.

"She pestered him," Bob said. "She kept pestering him until she had a hold on him. That's why he killed Gert."

"You're a liar," Madge said. "He killed Gert because he hated her. And that's why he'll kill me. He hates me."

"He doesn't hate you," Bob said. "Nobody hates you. You're not the type that makes people hate. You only make people annoyed. He didn't know he was annoyed. He didn't have the brains to see it. He was ignorant and he's still ignorant. If he wasn't ignorant he wouldn't have killed Fellsinger. He wouldn't have come to San Francisco in the first place. Now it's a cinch they'll give him the chair."

"That's makes me scared," Madge said. "He knows he's going to get the chair. He knows he has nothing to lose now. When it gets like this they go out of their mind. They don't care what they do. That's why I'm afraid to be alone. He'll find me. He'll look for me until he finds me."

"He won't look for you," Bob said. "I know how it is with him."

"How is it with him?" Irene said.

"It's a matter of psychoanalysis," Bob said. "The power of suggestion, and a bit of the identification process. Like this—she managed to get a hold on him, and she increased that hold to the point where he thought he wanted her more than anything else. Because he was weak and ignorant, he looked for the easiest way to get rid of Gert. He thought the easiest way was murder. Now he identifies her with trouble. He'll stay away from her."

"What do you know about psychoanalysis?" Madge said. "What do you know about these things? You never had any brains yourself. All you know is T squares and drawing boards and you don't even know much about that. What are you? You're nothing."

"Yes, I know that," Bob said. "We've been through that before. A couple hundred thousand times. A couple hundred thousand years ago, when I was a monkey and I didn't know that the only way to stop hearing that voice of yours was to walk so far away that I wouldn't be able to hear it."

"I could say plenty," Madge said.

"That's very true," Bob said. "Your mouth is the greatest piece of machinery I've ever seen. Even if Parry is already out of his mind he'll have enough sense to stay away from that mouth of yours. You'd not only talk him out of killing you, you'd talk him into taking up with you again."

"You're a dirty liar," Madge said. "He never had anything to do with me."

"And Santa Claus has nothing to do with Christmas," Bob said. "Listen, Madge, I got out of kindergarten a long time ago. And I only sleep eight hours a day. The rest of the time my eyes are wide open. And my hearing is perfect. Put it together and what have you got?"

"Either you're lying," Madge said, "or someone was lying to you."

"Gert wasn't a liar," Bob said. "She was many other things but she wasn't a liar."

"She lied," Madge said. "She lied, she lied —"

"Every word she said was God's honest truth," Bob said. "And don't sit there with your eyes bulging out as if you can't make head or tail of it. Will you deny that he went to your apartment?"

"What?"

"What. What. What. Listen to her."

Irene's voice came into it, part confusion, yet somewhat firm. "Bob, please — don't be a cad."

"I want her to know, Irene. I want her to know I'm not the fool she thinks I am. She thinks I was in the dark all the time she was hiring someone to watch me."

"I never did that," Madge said.

"All right, you never did that. Except if I wanted to go

to the trouble I could prove that you did. Because I got hold of the little rat you hired. And I asked him what you were paying. And I offered him double the amount to keep an eye on you. The very next day he made good. He came back and told me there was a man in your apartment the night before. He told me the man stayed about four hours."

"He's a liar, you're a liar—"

"Everybody's a liar," Bob said. "But it's amazing the way all these lies fit together and click, like a key opening a lock. Because he told me he followed the man from your apartment. He followed the man home. And home was the apartment house where the Parrys lived. If you want me to go further I'll go further. He gave me a description of the man. I had never seen Parry but Gert told me what Parry looked like. And you know what I did? I put it down in black and white, with the date and time and everything. And I had this little rat sign a statement, and if I wanted to I could have used that statement. But I didn't and I'll tell you why. I felt sorry for Parry. I even felt sorry for Gert."

"You kept that signed statement?" Irene asked.

"Yes."

"Why didn't you bring it up at the trial?" Irene asked. "Why didn't you give it to Parry's lawyer?"

"I don't see what good it would have done," Bob said. "It would have only made things worse for him. And it would have implicated me. I didn't want any part of it. I knew Parry was guilty anyway and I knew he didn't have a chance to prove otherwise."

"It's all a lie," Madge said. "The whole thing is one big lie. Don't fall for it, honey. He's only trying to paint me bad."

"Madge, you're not bad," Bob said. "You're just a pest."

Madge began to sob.

Irene said, "Bob, you shouldn't say things like that."

Madge said, "What he says doesn't bother me. It's just

141

that I'm so scared."

Irene said. "I think you ought to go now, Madge."

"I won't go home alone."

"Take her home, Bob."

"Not me. I don't want to have anything to do with her."

Madge was sobbing loudly.

Irene said, "Madge, I'm going to call a taxi."

"All right," Madge said, and she stopped sobbing. "Call a taxi. And after I'm gone you can turn on the phonograph." Her voice was stiff now, with all the sobbing out of it, with something else in it that had the shape in sound of a blade. "Turn it on loud so you can hear it in the bedroom."

Then everything was quiet. And everything was waiting.

It lasted for the better part of a minute.

Then Bob said, "Would you mind explaining that last remark?"

"Does it need explaining?" Madge said. She put something of a laugh into it.

"I think so," Bob said. "Because I haven't the faintest idea of what you're talking about."

"Your memory can't be that bad," Madge said. "Don't tell me you can't remember back to yesterday afternoon."

"What about yesterday afternoon?" Bob said.

"I came here to see Irene. I might as well get this out here and now. I came here to see her. She wouldn't answer the buzzer. I knew she was home. I was curious. So I used the fire-escape exit and came up here and knocked on the door. There wasn't any answer and I was ready to think I had made a mistake and she wasn't home after all. But I could hear the phonograph going. That meant she was in and she didn't want to answer the door. She was in here with you. Yesterday afternoon."

Everything was quiet again.

It lasted for a good ten seconds.

Then Bob said, "It wasn't me, Madge."

"Then it was someone else," Madge said.

Bob laughed. It was a mild laugh yet it was sort of twisted. He said, "Of course it was someone else. You know that. You made sure of it yesterday afternoon when you called up the place where I work, when you asked to speak to me. You must have called from the drugstore on the corner, right after you left here. And as soon as I got on the phone and you heard my voice you hung up. I was wondering about that call. I've been wondering about it until now."

"But someone was up here," Madge said. "I heard the phonograph going."

"That's very true," Irene said. "The phonograph was going and someone was in here with me."

"A man?" Bob said.

"Yes, Bob. It was a man."

"Who was it?" Bob said. His voice was all twisted.

Seconds dragged through quiet. Then Irene said, "Vincent Parry."

CHAPTER 14

Parry was standing near the door. His eyes were taking his body through the door but his feet were staying where they were and pulling his body back. The itching under the bandage was a moist itching that made little pools of itching all over his face. And the little pools became jagged here and there and they had facets that contained more itching. He couldn't feel air going through the hole in the bandage in front of his mouth and he couldn't feel himself breathing. The quiet from the other room got through the door and shaped itself around him and began to crush him. He thought it was because he wasn't breathing. He knew he could breathe if he wanted to but he didn't want to because he knew, if any air came into his mouth and down into his lungs he was going to let it out in a shout. This thing happening now was what he had expected, what he had expected would happen sooner or later, when she finally realized she couldn't keep it up, so sooner or later she must come out with it. So now she was out with it, taking herself away from it as it came out. And now he was alone again, and he couldn't take himself away from it as she could. He was alone with it, and she was going away from it, and it was part of the quiet that crushed him now. And he was alone, crushed by it. And he knew as long as he was alone he mustn't be alone here. Turning and staring at the window he could see the roof tops of San Francisco forming a high, jagged wall that stared back at him and solemnly dared him to get past, and telling him what a difficult time it would be, what a complex time, what a lonely time he would have of it. Sliding back at him now, coming back like a wheeled thing on greased rails, bouncing away from a cushioned barrier, was the memory of a night when Madge had almost captured him, when her arms were tight around his middle and he was standing there looking past her shoulder at the window and a San Francisco night beyond. And wanting to twist away from her but not being able to twist away, and he had to stand there and listen as she told him that he was not happy with Gert, he would never be happy with Gert. With Gert his life amounted to one agony after another, with Gert he was only a tool that Gert picked up at widely spaced intervals, but with Madge he would be a permanent necessity and why couldn't he understand that he was fortunate to be wanted so badly. While she talked he talked silently back to her, admitted to her that she was gradually selling him a carload of merchandise, talked to himself and asked himself what he was going to do with that merchandise once he had it. She talked on, throwing arguments at him, and they were sound arguments, anyway they sounded sound, and he was telling himself that he might as well go ahead and try it out, he didn't have anything to lose. His life with Gert was one big headache, and if Madge lived up to a fraction of the things she was promising now, it might be a good idea to take the gamble and let her complete the sale. And then he wanted to get his hands free so he could light a cigarette, and as he pulled his arms away from Madge he heard a grinding

145

gasp and it was Madge, gasping again, backing away from him, asking him why he had pulled away like that. He said he only wanted to light a cigarette. She hurled herself at a sofa, sobbing loudly, saying that a cigarette was more important to him than a woman who wanted him more than she wanted to breathe. She wriggled convulsively on the sofa and all at once she sat up and showed him a wet face and she wanted him to tell her why so many other things were more important to him than herself. He found himself trying to explain that these so many other things weren't really more important, they were merely little conveniences that a man had to have every now and then. Every now and then a man had to take time out to light a cigarette or grab a drink of water or walk around the block or stand alone in a dark room.

Madge refused to accept that. Madge said it wasn't fair for him to go for that cigarette just when they were about to put their two lives together and make one out of it. And just then he realized what a great mistake it would be to go along with Madge. They would never get in step because she would never allow him to follow his own plans. She had to be in on everything. She had to be the captain, and even if he went ahead and handed her the captaincy she would find something wrong with that. She would turn the captaincy over to him and when he took it she would find something wrong with that and she would take a jump at the sofa and start that wriggling and sobbing. He told himself she really wasn't such a bad person, she was just a pest, she was sticky, there was something misplaced in her make-up, something that kept her from fading clear of people when they wanted to be in the clear. He felt uncomfortable just looking at her there on the sofa. That was it precisely. In the same room with her he would never be comfortable.

He told her that. He put the blame on his own shoulders, saying he was one of these selfish specimens and he could never give her the attention she was looking for. She came leaping from the sofa, crying loudly he was all wrong, they would really click, they really would, and let them have the courage to take a shot at it, and please, Vincent, please, and she had her arms around him again, and his resistance was flowing away. If she wanted him that badly maybe he ought to give it a try despite all the reasons against it. He wanted to smoke a cigarette and think it over and again he tried to get free of her arms and the feel of her arms was like a chain and frantically he wanted to get away.

His head turned and again he was looking at the window. He knew he had to take a chance with that window. He moved toward it.

He heard Bob Rapf saying, "You're very funny, Irene."

Irene said, "What's funny about it?"

Madge said, "What was Vincent Parry doing here?"

"He came to here to kill me," Irene said.

"Hilarious," Bob said.

"Well," Madge said, "what happened?"

"I talked him out of it," Irene said.

"Aw," Bob said, "for Christ's sake."

"I'm afraid to be alone," Madge said.

"Keep quiet, Madge." Again Bob's voice was twisted. "Listen, Irene, I think before I go you should tell me who was really here yesterday."

"I told you."

"All right," Bob said. "I think I understand. This is the final stop, isn't it?"

"I'm afraid so," Irene said. "I should have told you before. But I didn't think it was serious with him. Yesterday he said it was serious. I don't know yet how it is with me. But I keep thinking about it and at least that's something. I think I ought to give it a chance."

"Who is he?" Bob said.

"Just another man. Nothing extraordinary."

"What does he do?" Bob said.

"He's a clerk in an investment security house."

"That's what Parry was," Madge said.

"Madge, why don't you keep quiet?" Bob said. "Irene, I want you to know I valued our friendship. I valued it highly. I hope things work out nicely for you."

"Thanks, Bob."

"Good-by, Irene."

"Are you going to call a taxi?" Madge said.

"No," Bob said. "We'll get a taxi outside. Where's your car?"

"It's getting fixed," Madge said. "Maybe we won't see a taxi."

"Keep quiet," Bob said. "Come on, I'll take you home."

"Good night, honey." Madge was starting to sob again. "I'll call you tomorrow morning."

"I'm going to be rather busy," Irene said.

"When should I call you?" Madge said.

"Well," Irene said, "I'm going to be rather busy from now on."

"Oh," Madge said. "Well, I'll get in touch with you in a couple of days. Or maybe I'll call you tomorrow night."

Bob said, "I'll tell you what to do, Irene. You pick up the sofa and throw it at her. Maybe that would make her understand. Come on, Madge."

The door opened and closed. The place was quiet. Parry leaned against a wall and looked at the floor. Minutes were sliding past and he was waiting for the bedroom door to open. He heard the sound of his breathing and it was a heavy sound. He was trying to get it lighter and he couldn't bring it down from the heaviness.

The bedroom door opened. Irene came in and walked to the window. She said, "They're going down the street.

They'll probably go to the traffic light intersection and get a taxi there." She turned and looked at Parry. She said, "Well?"

He shook his head slowly.

"If you were in there," Irene said, "if you had seen their faces, you'd know I handled it right. I had to be funny. I couldn't work on Madge alone. And I had to be delicate with Bob. Now he won't bother me and he won't let her bother me."

He kept on shaking his head. And he was waiting for the buzzer to sound again. He was waiting to hear the voice of Bob Rapf, demanding to see the bedroom, to search the place. He was waiting for Studebaker and the police. He was waiting to hear the voice of Madge Rapf, asking if it was really Parry who had been here yesterday afternoon.

Then yesterday was yesterday no longer. Yesterday was two days ago.

And yesterday was three days ago. He went through four magazines and dreadful itching under the bandage and waiting for her to come in, and taking the food through the glass straws. And smoking up pack after pack of cigarettes.

And yesterday was four days ago and the itching was unbearable and the waiting was without time, without measurement. There were no calls. There were no visitors, no buzzing, nothing, only the food through the glass straws and the itching, the endless itching, and his wrists tied to the bedposts at night, and orange juice through the glass straws in the morning, and the waiting, and alone in the afternoon waiting for her to arrive with the food and the magazines and the cigarettes and the papers. In the papers, it was no longer on the front page. The column was shrinking. The headline was in smaller face type now, and they were saying they were still looking for him but that was all. And she had a new dress. And he wondered why there was no buzzing, why there were no visitors. He wondered what happened to Studebaker. He couldn't see any car out there now. He wondered why he was still afraid of Studebaker when there was no Studebaker out there now.

Then yesterday was five days ago.

It was raining again.

It was raining very hard, and he heard the rain before he opened his eyes. As he knocked his fist against the side of the bed to bring her in so she could untie his wrists, he was turning his head and looking at the rain coming down. The door opened and she was in the doorway, saying good morning and asking him if he had slept well, then putting a cigarette in the holder, lighting a match for him.

The itching under the bandage was a soggy itching, and it remained that way all through the day, and in the early evening it was a flat itching, without the burning, as it if was going away, as if it was smoothing out and going away from itself. The bandage felt very loose, getting looser every hour, and it was as if the bandage was telling him now it was ready to come off, now he didn't need it any more.

He was glad the time had come to take the bandage off, he was afraid to take the bandage off, he sensed the itching going away finally and completely, actually felt it walking away as he sat there on the sofa a few hours after dinner, as he sat there with a cigarette in the holder and the holder in his mouth, as he looked at Irene sitting across the room. She was reading a magazine, and she looked up and looked at him. He looked at his wrist watch. It said ten twenty. Coley had said five days. And at four thirty it would be exactly five days. He had six hours to go until it would be five days. He was sitting there wearing the grey worsted suit with the suggestion

150

of violet in it and he was waiting for another hour to go by. Then the hour was behind him and it was five hours to go until it was five days. Under the bandage his face felt dry and flat and smooth. He picked up a magazine. It was a picture magazine and it showed him a girl in a bathing suit, on tiptoe with her arms flung out toward the sea, with the waves rolling in toward the smooth beach where she stood, and his face felt smooth like the beach looked, and the girl wore a flower in her hair which was blond, very blond though not as blond as the hair Irene wore sort of long so that it sprayed her shoulders, where it was very yellow against the yellow upholstery of the chair on the other side of the room. The girl in the bathing suit was slim but not as thin as Irene, who was very thin there on the other side of the room where she sat wearing a yellow dress, light and loose, and yet not as light and loose as the bandages on his face.

He closed his eyes. He let his head sag, let the magazine slide from his fingers, and he knew he was going to stride halfway toward sleep and stay there, dangling at the halfway point, and she couldn't wake him up. She would let him stay there, half asleep until it was four thirty, until it was time to get the bandage off. Now he could feel his face separated from the bandage, knowing it was new and ready under the bandage, all ready with the bandage so loose and air in there and everything dry and fresh and ready. And clean, like the clean shirt he wore, and new, like the new tie, and ready as his body was ready, ready to get moving and go away. And he thought of Patavilca, and he thought of George Fellsinger and he thought of the money remaining in the pocket of the grey worsted suit. Almost eight hundred dollars, and it was enough, very much enough. It was enough for food and lodging and railroad tickets. Down through Mexico, down through Guatemala, Honduras, Nicaragua, Costa Rica. Down through Panama. Or perhaps he could fly. It would be better to fly. It would be swift and luxurious. Down through Mexico. Past them all and down through Colombia and Ecuador. Down to Peru, landing in Lima, then going up to Patavilca, staying in Patavilca, staying there for always. And the things he had seen in the travel folder were spreading out, going out very wide, and now immense, and moving in all the dimensions, the water purplish out there away from the bright white beach, the water moving, the waves coming in, smooth under the sun, smooth as his face was smooth, smooth under the bandage.

He wondered who had killed George Fellsinger.

The money would last long in Patavilca. American money always lasted long down there in those places, and after he made certain arrangements with papers he would find work and gradually he would learn to speak Spanish, learn to speak it the way they spoke it down there and would have something to start with, something to build from, something that would grow by itself even as he kept building it.

He wondered about his health. The kidney trouble. The sinus.

He would be all right if he watched himself, and if he did have attacks now and then he knew how to handle these attacks and he would be all right. He would be all right in Patavilca. He would be fine down there, and he wondered if they had cigarettes down there, and he wondered what Peruvian cigarettes tasted like, and wondered if he would see a woman down there who would be very thin, very graceful with the thinness. He decided that after a while when his Spanish was all right he would open up a little shop and sell the things they needed down there. He could make trips to Lima and buy things and bring them up and sell them in the shop. He wouldn't work hard. He wouldn't need to work hard. He would have everything he

152

needed and would really have everything he wanted. And it would be delightful down there in Patavilca.

He wondered why anyone would want to kill George Fellsinger.

It there was anything wrong with the Patavilca idea, it was only that he would be alone down there. But wherever he went he would be alone because he couldn't afford to take up with anyone. Sooner or later that someone would begin asking questions that had no direct answer and it would lead to a puzzle and that someone would want to solve the puzzle. So Patavilca was logical after all, and he was glad it was logical because it was the place where he wanted to be, because he so much liked what he had seen in the travel folder, and he had seen many travel folders, many pictures of many places and he had never seen anything quite like Patavilca. So he was glad it was going to be Patavilca after all, and when he was down there for a while maybe he wouldn't be alone after all because then he would be speaking Spanish and he would get to know Peruvians and there would be things to talk about and places to see and he would have everything he wanted in Patavilca. He wouldn't get too friendly with anyone, but he would know just enough people to prevent himself from getting lonely.

He wondered if things had happened in the Fellsinger case that weren't in the papers.

And in Patavilca they would never get him. For the rest of his life he would be away from them. He saw something that had happened long ago. It was when he was in Oregon to see that basketball game. That day when he arrived up there it was snowing in Eugene. He was in his room in a little hotel and outside it was gradually clearing but there was much snow. A little bus came down the street. There were some children playing on the sidewalk and they were making snowballs. As the bus passed them they threw snowballs at the windows. He remembered one of the children was wearing a bright green sweater and a bright green wool cap. And the bus was bright orange, and as the snowballs hit the windows the driver let loose with the exhaust that caused a minor explosion, a spurt of black smoke that frightened the children and sent them scampering away. But they were away and that was what they wanted. And he would be away and that was what he wanted. The spurt of black exhaust smoke was the futile attempt to grab him, but it wasn't enough to grab him and in Patavilca he would be away. He would be away from everything he wanted to be away from.

He wondered why someone had killed Gert. He wondered why that someone had killed George Fellsinger.

In Patavilca he would be under the sun most of the time, letting the sun pour down on him, on the beach under the sun, walking into the purplish water. Perhaps it was really and fully as purplish as it had looked in the travel folder.

A hand nudged his shoulder. He looked up. He saw her. She said, "Vincent—it's time."

He brought his head back. She was smiling.

She said, "It's four thirty. It's time to take the bandage off."

He looked at his wrist watch. It said four thirty.

She went into the bathroom. She came out with a pair of scissors. He began to quiver. His face felt very dry and flat and smooth and ready under the bandage. The bandage was soggy and old and his face felt new.

She started to cut the bandage. She worked slowly. She sat there with his face brought forward a little so she could get at the bandage better. Now the bandage was coming off. It came off smoothly, easily, and she unwrapped the gauze until she came to more adhesive tape, then she went through that with the scissors and unwrapped more gauze.

He watched her. She didn't see his eyes. She had her attention centered on the bandage, getting it away from his mouth, now going up past his cheeks and his nose, and he watched her, and her face wouldn't tell him anything, and she had it coming away from the upper part of his face and then she took hold of it where it was caked and very slowly she pulled it away so that now she had the entire bandage off. And she had it in her hands, with the scissors and she was looking at him. She was looking at his new face.

And then she fainted.

CHAPTER 15

It was quiet and very slow, the way she went down, the way she subsided on the floor. She looked tired and little there, and now he was not yet starting to wonder why she had fainted. He only felt sorry for her because she had fainted. He went into the bathroom and took hold of a glass and turned on the cold water faucet. Then he realized there was a mirror in front of him, level with his face. And he looked up.

And he saw his new face.

He frowned.

It was very difficult to believe that he was actually looking at himself. This was not himself.

This was new and different and he had not expected this. The shape of his face was changed. The aspect of his face was all changed. He still had the same eyes and nose and lips, unchanged, but they seemed to be placed differently.

There was nothing dreadful about it. There was everything remarkable and fascinating about it. The man who had fixed his face was a magician. He wondered why Irene had fainted. He leaned toward the mirror. There were no scars, except when he made extremely close study he could see the faint outlines. Only five days ago, and it was astounding. There was nothing in the mirror to indicate that he had been given a new face, but his former face had undergone an operation and new flesh had been added and steel had gone into the flesh and his face had been changed. There were no signs of damage, there was nothing except the new face. He could see it under the five-day beard, the pale, scattered growth.

And he wondered why she had fainted.

He leaned even closer toward the mirror. And he examined his new face. He twisted his features and his features twisted nicely, as if he had always owned this face. He put his hands to his face and it was really his face. In the mirror he saw his hands on his face and on his face he felt the pressure of his hands and there was no pain, there was no special feeling. Only his hands on his new face.

Perhaps the beard had something to do with it. But he didn't have much of a beard, and his face was distinct under what beard there was. The beard hadn't caused it. He wondered what had caused it, what had caused her to faint.

He filled the glass with cold water, went into the living room. He dipped fingers into the glass, flicked water on her face. She opened her eyes. She started to sit up. She looked at his face and shuddered and closed her eyes again. He flicked more water, and she opened her eyes, sat up fully. She looked at him. Her eyes stretched up and down.

He said, "Is it as bad as that?"

His voice was different.

He said, "It's all right with me. And if it's all right with me it ought to be all right with you."

His voice was very different. It had always been a light voice. Now it was even lighter, and it was somewhat hollow.

She stood up. She was looking at him. She said, "I expected to see something very dreadful."

"Is that why you fainted?"

She nodded. She couldn't stop the up-and-down stretching of her eyes. She said, "I guess it was everything, added up. I'm sorry."

He didn't know what to say. He mumbled, "I guess these things happen sometimes."

"Take the whiskers off," she said. "Maybe I'm imagining things."

He went into the bathroom. He looked at the face again. Then he prepared it for shaving. The skin cream felt all right, the soap felt all right. Even the razor felt all right. And afterward the cold water felt like cold water always feels. He mopped the towel against the face and then he looked at the face. It was bright and new and clean. He wondered what had happened to the flesh that had been taken from his arms. He couldn't see any sign of it on his new face. And on his arms the cuts had healed, had been healed now for two days. And he had a new face, and already he was beginning to feel that he had always owned this face. And it was magic.

He went into the living room, buttoning his shirt.

She looked at him. Now he was arranging his tie. She said, "Yes, it's unbelievable."

"Are you going to let it get you?"

"I don't know what I'm going to do."

"You have no problem," he said. "I'm all right now. I can go now. You don't need to worry about it any more."

She looked at the window. Out there it was coming down from overturned tubs. The wind was hitting it and throwing it all around out there and it was one of those very big rains that come down now and then from the north, pushed by a wild and warm wind.

She said, "When are you going?"

"Now."

"No."

"I can't stay here."

"Where will you go?"

"I don't know."

"I can't stay here either," she said.

"Why not?"

"I just feel that I can't, that's all."

"I don't get this."

"Neither do I. But it's the way I feel. I just can't stay here. I've got to go away somewhere."

He picked up a pack of cigarettes. She wanted one. He lit her cigarette and lit his own. He looked at the window. He said, "All right, Irene. Give me it. All of it."

"Beginning with what?"

"Your father." He walked toward the window. He examined the thickness and speed of the rain. He turned and looked at her.

She said, "He didn't kill my stepmother. It was an accident. That's what he said. That's what I believed and what I'll always believe. And I'll always believe that you didn't kill your wife and you didn't kill George Fellsinger."

"With Gert and Fellsinger it was no accident. Somebody killed them."

"It wasn't you."

"Then who was it?"

"I don't know."

He sat on the sofa and made little burning orange circles with the end of the cigarette. He said, "Maybe it was Madge."

"Maybe."

"Maybe it was Bob Rapf."

"Maybe."

He stopped playing with the cigarette. He put it in his mouth and gave it a pull. He let the smoke come out slowly and he looked at her and said, "Maybe it was you."

She came over to the sofa and sat at the other end. She leaned back and her eyes went toward the ceiling. She said, "Maybe."

Parry took another pull at the cigarette. He said, "I don't know why I'm trying to figure it out. I don't see what difference it makes now. I don't want to get even with anybody. All I want is to get away. I've got my new face and nobody will recognize me, and I ought to be getting on my way while the getting is good."

"But you're curious, aren't you?"

"I guess that's it," he said. "I guess I'm beginning to get curious."

"And angry."

"No," he said. "No, I'm not angry. I thought all along it was an accident that killed Gert. Now that I know it was murder I ought to be angry. But I'm not.

I'm not even angry about Fellsinger. I'm sort of sad about Fellsinger but not too sad because he didn't have much to live for anyway. What I can't understand is why anyone would want to kill him."

"And your wife?"

"That's easier."

"Well," she said, "that's something. Start from there."

"No. I'll let it stay where it is and I'll go away from it. I've had enough of it. I've got to get away."

"Maybe if you tried you could find something."

He looked at her. He studied the grey eyes and said, "Do you really want me to try?"

"If you think it's worth it, yes. If you think you've got something to start with, a place to start, and a time, and if you can work from there—"

"Yes," he said, still studying the grey eyes. "I've got a place and a time. The place was that road. The time was the moment you followed me into those woods."

"Take it back further. Take it back to the trial. Do you see any logic in the fact that I was more than a little interested in the trial?"

He looked at the floor. "How sure are you that your father was innocent?"

"Just as sure as I know you're innocent. Just as sure as I know there's a world and a sun and stars. I reacted normally when I recognized the similarity between your situation and what happened to my father. I couldn't get in on your trial but I knew it was an accident, just as my stepmother's death was an accident. All I could do was write crazy letters to the *Chronicle*."

He nodded. "That was all right then." He shook his

head. "Now there's no similarity. There's a killer in this somewhere."

"You're not a killer, Vincent."

He frowned. "That can't be the only reason you're going to bat for me. There's another reason dancing around in the middle of all this and now that we're having a showdown you might as well hand it over."

She didn't reply to that immediately.

He watched her.

A good fifteen seconds went by. Then she said, "I'm helping you because I feel like helping you. Do you mind?"

"No," he said. "I'm too tired to mind. I'm too tired to coax it out of you. But every now and then I'll think about it. Maybe I'll even worry about it. I don't know. Let's play some Count Basie."

"Nothing doing." Abruptly her voice was firm. "You don't want to hear Basie just now. You want to hear all about the hook-up. Madge, and myself — and Bob."

He remembered a phrase used by the little man, Max Weinstock, the upholsterer. He said, "Just one of those things."

"No, Vincent. Not just one of those things. San Francisco is a big city. When the trial ended I wasn't satisfied. I knew there were things that hadn't come out in the courtroom. I wanted to get at those things. There's a certain gift some people have for getting to meet people and striking up friendships. I'm either blessed or damned with that gift, because only a few weeks after the trial ended I was friendly with Madge Rapf."

"Did she know what you were after?"

"If she did, if she had the slightest idea, she ought

162

to get an Academy Award. No, Vincent, I'm sure I managed it all right. We were seeing a lot of each other, lunch and shopping and movies and so forth, and it got to the point where I could write her biography if I wanted to."

"Would there be a chapter on me?"

"Not more than a paragraph, if Madge had her way. She painted you as a liar and a rat and a murderer. She said you made a tremendous play for her and not only her but anything you came across in a cocktail bar."

"Well?"

"It's all right, Vincent. I'm pretty sure I know the way it was. She pestered you and you didn't want any part of her so she finally gave it up. That's what I got from Madge, even though she put it the other way around. I guess we really shouldn't blame her too much. The old pride angle. When a woman loses everything else she can keep on going as long as she holds onto her pride. Or spirit. Or whatever you want to call it."

"Okay," Parry said. "Let's sit here and feel sorry for Madge."

Irene smiled. "You know, it's odd. I ought to get irritated. I ought to get irritated at a lot of things you say. Or maybe it's because I know what you really mean to say. You say we should sit here and feel sorry for Madge and what you really mean is we should sit here and check Madge off the list and get onto Bob."

Parry started toward the window, changed his mind, went over to the radio-phonograph and ran fingers along the glazed yellow surface. He said, "When does Bob come into it?"

"About a month or so after I became friendly with Madge. Of course she told me all about him, what a cad he was, what a beast, what a skunk, and I think she went at least halfway through the zoo. I saw a way of maneuvering the situation and when I saw his name in the telephone book I did a very rotten thing. I called him up and told him I was a friend of Madge's and I was curious to see what he looked like and what he amounted to. He was peeved at first but I put some comedy into it and after some twenty minutes of fencing he agreed to give me a dinner date. I told Madge about it and she got a kick out of it and later I told her about the dinner date and she got a kick out of that, too. But then when there were more dates and she walked in on one of them she stopped getting a kick out of it. She saw I was having a definite effect on Bob and that was when she began to bother me. You know, the subtle approach. An insinuation here and there, a dig, a statement that I could take two ways. She never came out in the open and demanded that I stop seeing Bob. That isn't her method. When I told Bob about it he said I shouldn't give it another thought. He said Madge is happy only when she is pestering people. He told me to get into the habit of shutting a door in her face, but I couldn't get myself to do that."

"Did Bob ever talk about Gert?" He wasn't sure why he was asking that.

"He said she was a plague. He said he pitied you."

"How did he know she was a plague? Did Madge tell him that?"

"No. That was his own opinion."

"Based on what? Maybe I'm going to find out

something. I didn't know Bob was closely acquainted with Gert."

"He was seeing her."

"Oh. So he was seeing her. You mean he admitted that?"

Irene nodded. "He was seeing a lot of her."

"Because he wanted to?"

"I can't say for sure. He didn't go into it with me."

"What do you think?"

"I think Gert was trying to lasso him."

"Let's come back to Madge. Did Madge know about Gert and Bob?"

"I asked Bob about that and he said no. He said he wasn't seeing Gert during the time Madge had that man watching him. There was no way Madge could know. They were meeting each other in out-of-the-way places. They were very careful."

"You mean Bob Rapf admitted that to you?"

"He admitted the technical side of it."

"The technical side," Parry murmured. "And did it give you anything to work with?"

"No," Irene said. "There wasn't enough of it. And it was only one side. Anyway, by that time I wasn't working on it any more. I was beginning to feel that there wasn't any way I could help you."

"Only one side," Parry murmured, again looking at the floor. "—only one side, and it's the technical side. All right, let's stay technical. Let's put it in numbers. Did he say how many times a week he was seeing Gert?"

"I didn't ask him that. I didn't see where it mattered."

"I don't see either. But I'm trying to see. During

165

those last two months before she died she was out three or four nights a week. I never asked where she went, because by that time I didn't give a hang where she went. I don't know, there could be an opening here. Three or four nights a week, and if I could know definitely she was spending all those nights with Bob Rapf I might have something."

"And what would you do with it?"

"I don't know. This sort of thing is out of my line. Those last two months. You see what I'm getting at? I want to know what she was doing those last two months. That's the keyhole, and now all I need is the key."

"I'm afraid that's out, Vincent. It's too late for the key."

"Because I'm in no position to go hunting?"

"Because the key is Gert. Only Gert could tell you what she was doing those last two months, those three or four nights a week when she was out. You can't build anything from what you've got now. You have no way of knowing there was anything important between Gert and Bob. Or Gert and anyone. So you can't do anything with that. You've got to find something else. Maybe if you could take yourself back to those last two months you could find something."

"Make it four months. The last four months. But there's nothing in that except trouble and heartache, knowing everything was ruined, the way she wouldn't let me touch her, the way she made me sleep in the living room those last four months. Were you there that day when they got that out of me?"

"Yes," she said. "I was there every day."

"And you remember when they asked me about

other women? You remember the way my lawyer objected and the prosecution claimed it was necessary to establish the factor of other women or perhaps one woman in particular, and you remember what I said?"

"I remember you said there was nobody special. You said you were with other women now and then. They asked you for the names of those other women and you said you didn't remember. The prosecution said it was impossible for you not to remember at least one or two of those names and you said you didn't even remember one. I knew you were lying. Everybody in that courtroom knew you were lying. You made a big mistake there, Vincent, trying to protect those other women, because you should have been thinking only of your own case. What you should have done was to say that you remembered but refused to give those names in public."

"I know," Parry said. "My lawyer bawled me out for it afterward. But afterward was too late. Anyway, it wouldn't have mattered. I didn't have a chance, no matter which way you look at it. And if I start with the what I should have dones and the what I should have knowns all I'll get out of it is a bad headache. My whole case was built around the theory that it was an accident, that she fell and hit her head on the ash tray. That was really the big mistake. But why go back to it? Why try to do anything about it? It's too late. It's much too late. I can't hang around even though I've got this new face, and besides I don't have the brains for that sort of thing. I don't know how to go about it. There's only one thing for me to do, and that's to get out of this town as fast as I can."

"You'll need more money."

"What you given me already is plenty."

"Where will you go?"

"I told you I don't know."

"You do know but you won't tell me."

"All right, I do know. Why should I tell you?"

She got up from the sofa. She walked across the room, turned when she came to the wall. She leaned against the wall. She said, "Do you think I'd ever change my mind? Do you think I'd ever let them know where you were?"

"You might."

"And that's why you won't tell me?"

"That's why."

"That's not why. You won't tell me because you think I'll come there. You think I'll follow you."

"You'd be crazy to follow me."

"Was I crazy to pick you up on that road? Was I crazy to let you stay here?"

"Yes."

"And if I was crazy enough to do that, I'd be crazy enough to follow you. Isn't that it?"

"I guess so. I don't know." He glanced at the wrist watch.

She took herself away from the wall. She folded her arms, as if she was standing in the cold. She looked very little, standing there. She said, "You do know. You know you could trust me. You know I'd never say anything. But you have a feeling I'd follow you if you told me where you were going. And you don't want me to do that. You don't want me there. You don't need me there. Isn't that the way it is?"

"I guess that's the way it is."

She smiled. She went into the bedroom. When she

came out there was money in her hand. She gave the bills to him, one at a time, and it added up to a thousand dollars.

He stood there with the money in his open hand. He said, "I really don't need this."

"You've got to have something. What you have isn't enough."

"All right, thanks." He put the money in his pocket.

She said, "Shall I call a taxi?"

"Please."

He felt light, he felt unfettered. She was going to call a taxi and he could walk out of here and get in a taxi and go wherever he wanted to go. He had his new face. He could do whatever he wanted to do. It was as if he had been stumbling along a clogged and muddy uncertain road, and all at once it branched off to become a wide and white concrete road, smooth and clean, and stretching away and away and away.

She was calling a taxi. He lit a cigarette.

She put the phone down. "Forty minutes," she said. "We'll have time for breakfast."

He smiled at her. She was a very dear friend. She was going to make breakfast for him. He said, "That'll be fine. I'm anxious to see."

"To see what?"

"How it feels to eat with a knife and fork."

She laughed brightly and went into the kitchen. He opened the lid of the phonograph. The black roundness was there, waiting for the needle. It was Basie again, the same Basie he had been using for the past four days, concentrating on the trumpet take-off, the wailing. It was *Sent For You Yesterday And Here You Come Today*. He turned the lever, lowered the needle, and there was the melancholy beginning, the rise of reeds and brass and the continued rise and the sudden break and Basie's right hand touching against not many keys but just the right keys. And he had almost eighteen hundred dollars in his pocket and he was very rich and he had this new face. And he was going to have a nice breakfast and then he was going to get in a cab and go wherever he wanted to go. And Basie was giving him just the right notes and everything was just right.

The record was ended. He played it again. He played it a third time. He selected another Basie. He kept on playing Basies until she called from the kitchen, telling him that breakfast was ready.

It was a very nice breakfast. The orange juice was just right, the scrambled eggs were just right, and the coffee. And he enjoyed using a knife and fork again. He enjoyed chewing on food, and the feeling of his new face.

He insisted on helping with the dishes. She let him dry them. They had cigarettes while they worked on the dishes. And when they were in the living room again they had more cigarettes. They were talking about Basie, they were talking about Oregon. She liked Oregon. She said the grass was a special shade of green up there. And she liked the lakes up there, the canoeing and the fishing and the hiking through country where there were no houses and everything was quiet and green for miles and miles. She had made many water colors of the Oregon country. She asked him if he would like to see some of her work. He said yes, and she went into the bedroom and he heard her searching for the paintings. Then she was coming into the living room and she had a large packet tied with string. She started to untie the string and the buzzer sounded.

She looked up. She said, "Your taxi."

"Yes."

The buzzer sounded again.

She said, "It sounds very final, doesn't it?"

"Yes."

"You're all right now, Vincent. They can't get you now."

"I'll need a new name."

"Let me give you a name. Even though you'll change it later let me give you one now. To go with your new face. It's a quiet face. Allan is a quiet name. Allan and — Linnell."

The buzzer sounded.

"Allan Linnell," he said.

"Good-by, Allan."

He was going toward the door. He turned and looked at her. She was all alone. He had a feeling she would always be alone. She would always be starved for real companionship.

The buzzer sounded again.

She would be all alone here in her little apartment. Her father was dead, her brother was dead, she really had nobody.

The buzzer sounded.

"Good-by," he said, and he walked out of the apartment.

The rain was flooding the street as he hurried toward the taxi. His eyes were riveted to the open door of the taxi. That was all he wanted to see. And when the door closed all he wanted to do was sit back and shut his eyes and shut his mind. But as the taxi started down the street he turned and looked through the rear window. He looked at the apartment house, at the third row of windows. And he saw something at one of the windows. He saw her standing there at the window, watching him go away.

The taxi took him to Civic Center. He got off on Market, went into an all-night diner and asked for a cup of coffee. He stayed with the coffee for twenty minutes. Last night's newspaper was on the counter and he picked it up and glanced at the front page. He began to turn the pages. He asked for another cup of coffee. He was on page seven. They were still wondering where he was. They gave him three inches and a single small headline that simply said he was still on the loose. There were no further developments. He looked at his wrist watch and it said six forty. He turned and looked through the grimy window of the diner. It was still raining very hard.

He felt uncomfortable. He told himself there was no reason why he should feel uncomfortable. All he had to do was wait around until nine o'clock, when the stores would open. Then he could go buy himself some clothes and things, and a grip, and he would be ready to check in at a hotel and make his arrangements from that point. Maybe by tonight he would already be on a train, or even a plane. He wondered why he was uncomfortable. He took his glance away from the newspaper and noticed there was a man sitting beside him. He remembered the man had been in the diner when he had come in. The man had been there at the far end of the counter. Now the man was sitting beside him.

The man was rolling a cigarette. He wore a swagger raincoat and a low-crown hat with a fairly wide brim. The cigarette wasn't rolling very well and the man finally gave it up and let the tobacco spill on the counter. Parry looked at the tobacco.

The man turned hi head and looked at Parry.

It was time to go. Parry started to slide away from the counter.

"Wait a minute," the man said.

Parry looked at the man's face. The face was past thirty years old. It featured a long jaw and not much eyes and not much nose. There was a trace of moustache.

"What's the matter?" Parry said. He kept going away from the counter.

"I saids wait a minute," the man said. It wasn't much of a voice. There was a crack in it, there was alcohol in it.

Parry came back to the seat. He looked at the spilled tobacco. He said. "What can I do for you?" He wondered if his face was changed sufficiently.

"Answer a few questions."

"Go ahead," Parry said. He tried a smile. It didn't give. He said, "I've got plenty of time." He wondered if that was all right. The man's face didn't tell him whether or not it was all right.

The man said, "What are you doing in this weather without a raincoat?"

"I'm absent-minded."

The man smiled. He had perfect teeth. He said, "Nup. Let's try it again."

"All right," Parry said. "I don't have a raincoat."

"That's better. We'll go on from there. Why don't

you have a raincoat?"

"I'm absent-minded."

The man laughed. He played a forefinger into the spilled tobacco. He said, "That's okay. That's pretty good. What are you doing up so early?"

"I couldn't sleep."

"Why not?"

"I'm not well. I have a bad kidney."

"That's tough," the man said.

"Yeah," Parry said. "It's no picnic. Well—" He started to get up.

"Wait a minute," the man said.

Parry settled himself on the seat. He looked at the man and he said, "What hurts you, mister?"

"My job," the man said. "It's a rotten job. But it's the only thing I know how to do. I've been at it for years."

"Are you on it now?"

"That's right."

"What do you want with me?"

"That depends. Let's have a few statements."

"All right," Parry said. "My name is Linnell. Allan Linnell. I'm an investment counselor."

"In town?"

"No." He grabbed at a town. He said, "Portland."

"What are you doing here?"

"Hiding," Parry said.

"From what?"

"My wife. And her family. And her friends. And everybody."

"Come on, now. It can't be that bad."

"I'll tell you what you do," Parry said. "You go up there and live with her for seven years. And then if

174

you're still in your right mind you come down here and tell me all about it."

The man shook his head slowly. He said, "I'm sorry, bud. I don't want to bother you like this, but it's my job. This town is very hot right now. All kinds of criminals all over the place. We got orders to check every suspicious personality. I'll have to see your cards."

"I don't have anything with me."

The man kept shaking his head. "You see? I've already started with you. I can't let it pass now. I'll have to take you in."

"I've got my wallet at the hotel," Parry said. "Couldn't we go over there? I'll give you all the identification you need."

"All right," the man said. "That'll make it easier. Let's go to the hotel."

Parry took some change out of his pocket, laid it on the counter.

They walked out of the diner, stood waiting under the sloping roof that kept the rain away from them.

"Where you staying?" the man said.

Parry tried to think of a place. He couldn't think of a place. He thought of something else. He looked at the man and he said, "I just remembered. The wallet's not there. I never keep my money in the wallet. The only thingkI took with me was money. All my available cash."

"How much?"

"Close to two thousand."

The man tapped a forefinger against his thin moustache.

Parry said, "I don't want to go back to Portland.

175

It's bad enough the way it is now. I'm just about ready to crack. I almost cracked a year ago and if I crack now I'll never get over it. And here's another thing. My name's not really Linnell. It's a new name because I'm trying to make a new start. I'll never make it if you take me in."

"You working now?"

"I only checked in last night," Parry said. "I'll find work. I know investments backwards and forwards."

The man folded his arms and watched the rain ripping down. He said, "What's the offer?"

"A hundred."

"Make it two."

Parry took bills from his pocket and began counting off fifties. He put four fifties in the man's hand.

The man studied the money and pocketed it and walked away.

Parry waited there for ten minutes. He saw an empty taxi, waved to it. The driver beckoned.

The taxi took him to Golden Gate Park, took him around the park and back to Civic Center. He went into a hotel lobby and bought a magazine and used up an hour. Then he went through the revolving door and stood under an awning and watched the rain weaken. When the rain had stopped altogether he walked down the street, kept walking until he came to a department store.

He bought a grip, a good-looking piece of yellow calf. He paid for it and told the salesman to hold it for him. Then he went over to the men's furnishings department and bought a suit and a thin raincoat. He bought shirts and shorts and ties and socks. He bought another pair of shoes. He was enjoying him-

176

self. He went into the toilet goods department and bought a toothbrush and a tube of toothpaste. He bought a razor and a tube of brushless shaving cream.

When he came back to the luggage department he told the salesman he wanted to put his purchases in the grip. He said it would be easier to carry them that way. The salesman said that was all right, as long as he had the receipts.

As he was leaving the department store a man came up to him and politely asked him if he had made any purchases. He said yes, and he showed the receipts. The man thanked him politely and told him to come again. He said he would, and he walked out of the store.

He looked for a hotel. He selected the Ruxton, a small place that wasn't fancy but was clean and trim. They gave him a room on the fourth floor. He was registered as Allan Linnell, and his address was Portland.

The room was small and very clean and neat. He gave the bellhop a quarter and when he was alone in the room he opened the grip, took out the packages and began to unwrap them.

The phone rang.

He looked at the phone.

The phone rang again.

He decided to let it ring.

It kept on ringing.

He sat down on the edge of the bed and stared at the phone.

The phone kept ringing and ringing.

He got up and walked across the room and picked up the phone.

He said, "Yes?"

"Room 417?"

"Yes?"

"Mr. Linnell?"

"Yes?"

"There's someone here to see you. May I send him up?"

It was a him. Then it had to be the detective. It had to be more money. The detective had trailed him, so it had to be more money or else the detective had changed his mind about taking the money and was going to take him in. He turned and saw three doors. One was a closet door, one was for the bathroom, one was for the corridor. He thought of the corridor, the fire escape. But if it was more money it would be all right. He thought of the fire escape. It was no good. It brought things back to a chase basis. He had to get rid of that. He had to end it before it became a chase.

"Mr. Linnell?"

"Yes, I'm still here."

"Shall I send him up?"

"Don't hurry me," Parry said, and he meant it. Again he thought of the fire escape. He told himself to stop thinking of the fire escape.

"Mr. Linnell?"

"Who is it wants to see me?"

"Just a moment, please."

Parry heard dim voices. The name wouldn't help, except that this gave him a few more seconds to think it over even though he knew there was nothing to think over.

"Mr. Linnell?"

"Yes?"

"It's a Mr. Arbogast."

Arbogast. It sounded hard, just as hard as the detective's face was hard. It had to be more money. And more money was all right and it had to be all right.

"Mr. Linnell?" The voice down there was impatient.

"All right," Parry said. "Send him up."

He put the phone down and went back to the bed and leaned against the post. It had to be more money, maybe another three hundred. And he could spare that. He told himself it would be all right after he gave the detective another three hundred and he told himself it wouldn't be all right because this was the second time. And as long as there was a second time there was the possibility of a third time. And a fourth and a fifth. And after his money ran out the detective would take him in. Again he began to consider the fire escape and this was the best time for the fire escape because the detective was already in the elevator and the elevator was going up. To use the fire escape he must use it now and right now.

Then he was moving toward the door, going slowly, telling himself to go faster, telling himself it was already a chase even though a chase was the last thing he wanted. He was trying to go faster and his legs wouldn't play along and he begged himself to go faster, to open the door and get out of here and give himself a lead and build the lead. He was almost at the door. He heard sounds in the corridor, footsteps coming toward the door. He felt empty and worn out, and he knew it was too late. If he ran now he would be up against a gun. All these detectives carried guns. A good idea for a novelty song. All detectives carry guns.

This was the end of it, because it couldn't be money, because it was a matter of plain reasoning, because the detective had already taken a big risk, taking that two hundred, and the detective had no intention of taking a bigger risk now. The detective was here to work, to give back the two hundred and take him in. There was a weakness in the wife in Portland story and the detective had snatched at the weakness before letting him get out of sight, and had trailed him and had him now and would take him in. And this was the end of it and it had to end this way, it had to end here, and what he had sensed all along was reality now, there was really no getting away, they had to grab him sometime, an ostrich could stick its head in the ground, stop seeing everyone else but that didn't mean they wouldn't see the ostrich. As he stood there listening to the footsteps coming toward the door he thought of how easy it had been at the beginning, how convenient everything had been, the way the truck was placed, the empty barrels in the truck, the guards away from the truck and the open gate and the truck going through. It had been very easy but it was ended now, and the ending of it was reasonable even though it wasn't fair, because now they would kill him, and he didn't deserve death.

The footsteps came closer and he wondered why it was taking so long for the footsteps to reach the door.

The sound of the footsteps was a soft mallet sound, softly tapping at the top of his skull, and slowly.

The sound of the footsteps took form and became a mallet. The mallet was a weapon. He ought to defend himself against a weapon. He had that right. It was proper and it was just that he should defend himself now. The mallet was the beginning of death and he had a right to defend himself against death.

The sound of the mallet was louder now, closer now, the feeling of it was heavier, and now it was fully upon him and it was hurting and he ought to think in practical terms, think of a way to defend himself. The detective was a fairly big man and the detective had a gun and fists wouldn't be sufficient. There was Patavilca to think of, there was getting away from here and going to Patavilca to think of, and the detective was trying to keep him away from that, trying to take him away from life and the delight of Patavilca and he had a right to defend himself, to hold onto life. He was looking at the door, listening to the footsteps coming toward the door, listening to the mallet, feeling the mallet, knowing that as each blow of the mallet came against him it was doing something to his brain, knowing he had to stop that, knowing he couldn't stop it, knowing he had a right to defend himself, listening to the footsteps, feeling the mallet, knowing it wasn't fair that they should kill him, knowing that soon it would be too late, he would be dead, and he was alive now, and he should be preparing to defend himself, knowing he was going to do something to defend himself, knowing he didn't hate the detective and he really didn't want to hurt the detective but he had to do something to defend himself and what he had to do was grab something. He turned his head and on the dresser across the room he saw an ash tray.

It was a glass ash tray.

It was fairly large.

It was heavy. A very heavy ash tray had killed Gert. This one was very heavy.

He stared at it.

The mallet was banging now, banging hard on his skull. He got up from the bed and went over and picked up the ash tray and he was thinking that he would open the door for the detective and hide the ash tray behind his back and manage to get behind the detective and then hit him with the ash tray, hit him hard enough so he would go down, hard enough so he would stay down, but not too hard, because too hard would kill the detective and he didn't want to kill the detective. He didn't want to but he wanted to hit the detective hard enough to put him down and keep him down long enough for the negotiation of the fire escape and the complete beginning of a complete getaway, but not too hard, of course not too hard. But hard enough. That would take measuring and he wondered if he would be able to measure it correctly. And he knew he wouldn't be able to measure it. He knew he was going to bring it down too hard because he was so anxious to get away, because now he was at a point where he was more afraid of bringing it down too lightly than too hard. And now that he had it in his hand and his mind was made up to use it he could not put it down and he was going to do something now that he didn't want to do, that he never expected he would do, and he didn't want to do it, and he pleaded with himself not to do it, and he knew he would always regret doing it, and he was sick and he was tired, every part of him was so tired except his right arm and his right hand and the fingers that had a firm hold on the heavy glass ash tray. He pleaded with himself to drop it, to let his fingers go limp, to let the ash tray go to the floor. His grip tightened on the ash tray, the mallet crashed down on him, the door became liquid, flowing toward him, flowing back, the floor was liquid, the door flowed in again, the mallet crashed down again, he saw it happening, just as if it was already happening he saw the detective coming in and the perfect teeth smiling at him and the forefinger tapping against the thin moustache and he heard the detective telling him it was tough and it was too bad but it was necessary to take him in and he could hear himself saying something about the offer of an extra three hundred and he could see the detective shaking a head and saying no, it was tough, it was too bad and it was a rotten job but it was a job all the same and it was necessary to take him in. And the detective was asking him to come along and he said all right, he would come along and then he was getting around and sort of behind the detective and the heavy glass ash tray was a part of his fingers, a part of his arm as he brought up his arm, brought it up high as the detective started to turn to look at him to see what he was doing and then he brought it down, swinging it down, the heavy glass ash tray, very heavy, very hard and thudding so horribly hard against the detective's head. And the detective stood there looking at him. And he wanted the detective to go down. And he brought the ash tray down again, and the head began to bleed. The blood came running out but the detective wouldn't go down so he hit the head again and still the detective wouldn't go down and he hit the head once more. And the detective refused to go down even though the blood was running very thickly now, very fast, and the ash tray came against the head and against the head again and the blood

183

washed down over the detective's face and the perfect teeth were smiling and very white and glistening until the blood dripped down over the teeth and made them very red and glistening and the detective stood there with his head of blood and he wouldn't go down.

The blood dripped onto the detective's shoulders, down over the detective's shoulders, down the arms, dripped off the ends of the fingers, dripped onto the floor, collected and pooled on the floor, rose up and clung to the detective's shoes, came up along the detective's trousers as more blood came down over the detective's chin, dripped onto the shirtfront and the detective was wearing a very red and glistening shirt and then a very red and glistening suit. All of the detective was red and glistening and the redness gushed from the black and deep openings in the detective's head and added to the glistening and the red. And the detective wouldn't go down. The detective was a glistening and red statue, all red, standing there and refusing to go down, and now it was impossible to use the ash tray again because the arm was tired, too tired to lift the ash tray again, and the detective stood there smiling with his perfect red teeth, and then there was a knocking on the door.

The redness stood there.

The knocking came again.

The redness vanished as Parry opened his eyes. Then he closed his eyes again, closed them tightly and tried to see redness or anything near redness and all he got was black. He opened his eyes and he heard the knocking, and he walked over to the dresser and put the ash tray back where it belonged. Then he walked back across the room toward the door, and with the

184

inside of his head a spinning vacuum he put a hand on the knob, knowing a crazy, careening joy as he anticipated the living face of the detective.

He opened the door and saw the face of Studebaker.

CHAPTER 16

There was no hat this time. There was grey hair, very thin on top. There was a new suit, a new shirt and a new tie. And new shoes. And Studebaker was smiling as he stood there in his new clothes. He put a hand in his coat pocket. He took out a small pistol and he pointed it at Parry.

He said, "Walk backward. Keep walking with your hands up until you hit the wall."

Parry walked backward. His shoulders came against the wall and he bounced a little and then he stood still with his hands up.

Studebaker was in the room now and he was closing the door. He had the pistol pointed at Parry's stomach. He said, "I could shoot you now and make myself five thousand dollars."

"I didn't know they were offering anything," Parry said.

"That's what they're offering," Studebaker said. "They're stumped."

"Have you talked to them?"

"No," Studebaker said. "If I was a dope I would've talked to them. I'm not a dope. In old clothes I know I look like a farmer but I'm not a farmer. Just stand there with your hands up and I'll stand here and we'll talk it over."

"What do you want?"

"Money."

"How much?"

"Sixty thousand."

"I can't afford that. I can't come anywhere near it."

"She can."

"Who?"

"The girl."

"What girl?"

"Irene Janney."

"Who's she?"

"Look, Parry. I told you I'm not a dope. And I'm not a farmer. I know she's worth a couple hundred thousand. She can spare sixty of it."

"She's out of it. You can't do a thing."

"Except turn you in. And that brings her in. That makes her an accessory to the Fellsinger job. It's twenty years off her life."

"They wouldn't give her that."

"All right, let's give her a break. Let's make it ten. It's still worth sixty thousand. That leaves her a hundred and forty thousand. With that hundred and forty she can get back the sixty in no time. And then we'll all be happy."

"No."

"You sure?"

"Yes," Parry said. "I'm sure." He watched the pistol. The pistol remained pointed at him but it was moving. Because Studebaker was moving, because Studebaker was going toward the phone.

Studebaker took hold of the phone and lifted it from the hook.

"Put it down," Parry said.

Studebaker smiled. He put the phone down. He said, "You'll play?"

"I'll think about it."

"That's okay. Think about it all you want to. Look at it up and down and sideways. You'll come to the same thing. You'll see it's the best way. What you've got to do now is shake me. I'm a big stone in the road and you've got to get rid of the stone to keep on going. So what you've got to do is talk to her and show her what her only move is. You got plenty on her."

"You too. You seem to know plenty."

"Not as much as you. If I went to her alone I wouldn't have much to back myself up. What I want to do is go there with you and have her see you with me so she'll know I'm not kidding. Then and there I want her to write me out a check for sixty thousand. That's the way we work it. We go there together."

"You've done this sort of thing before, haven't you?"

"Nup. This is the first time. How am I doing?"

"You're doing fine. Tell me, Arbogast, what are you?"

"I'm a crook."

"Small time?"

"Until now."

"In old clothes you don't look like a crook."

"In old clothes I look like a farmer."

"What will you do with the sixty thousand?"

"Probably go to Salt Lake City and open up a loan office. There's a fortune in it. People are crazy these days. People are always crazy but these days they're especially bughouse. They're making money but they want more. They're spending like lunatics. With a loan office I'll clean up. The way I got it figured out, sixty thousand gives me a perfect start."

"You won't keep bothering her, will you?"

"I tell you sixty thousand is just the right amount. I'll have it doubled and redoubled inside a couple years."

"Okay if I light a cigarette?"

"No. Keep your hands up."

"You're a careful guy."

"Sure I'm careful. I'm no dope. I'm careful and I'm smart. I'll give you a slant on how smart I am. I'll tell you the way I handled it, and then you'll know just how much of a chance you've got to put something over on me. Now you remember when I picked you up on that road, you remember you were wearing a pair of grey cotton trousers and heavy shoes and nothing more."

"You knew who I was right away."

"I didn't know anything of the kind," Arbogast said. "You had Quentin written all over you, but that was all. So I said to myself here's a fellow making a break from Quentin. I said to myself I'll pick up this fellow and see what he has to offer."

"That," Parry said, "I don't get."

"I'll tell you how it is with me," Arbogast said. "I'm always on the lookout for an opportunity. Anything that comes along with a possibility tag on it I grab. Here you were, out on the road, a fellow running away from Quentin. Maybe you had connections. Maybe you'd be willing to pay for a lift and a hiding place. Maybe I could stretch it out long enough to get something on you and shake you down later. That's the way I figured it. We'll say it was twelve to five I could make myself some heavy money on the deal. Twelve to five is always good enough for me, especially when my only bid is picking you up and having a talk with you. Now let's be agreeable and keep our hands up."

"They're up."

"Get them up higher and keep them that way. And maybe you better turn around. Yeah, I think you better turn around and face the wall and I'll see what you got."

Parry turned and faced the wall, holding his hands high. Arbogast came over and in four seconds checked him for a gun.

Then Arbogast stepped back. "So that was what I had in mind. But you pulled something I wasn't ready for and that made things tough for me. Not too tough, because I wasn't out cold when you got in the car with that girl. I saw the car going away and at first I didn't know what to make of it. But I'm no dope. That was a classy-looking car and there had to be money behind it. So I took the license number in my head. I got a good head for that sort of thing.

You beginning to see the way I had it laid out?"

"I'm beginning to see you're a man who plans for the future."

"Always," Arbogast said. "Anything that looks like it might lead to something. A fellow's got to be a few moves ahead of the game. It's the only way to get along in this world. Well, I had that license number in my head but I was in my underwear and I knew I couldn't go far that way. But you left your grey pants there and they fitted all right and I was wearing a sleeveless jersey and I still had my socks and shoes so that was all right, too. So I got in the car with that license number in my head and I made a U-turn and went back down the road aways and took another road. There was nothing for me to worry about because all my cards were in the Studebaker and if they stopped me and asked questions I could tell them I had a fall and banged up my face. But it didn't matter, I wasn't stopped. I took a roundabout way to Frisco and when I got in town I made a telephone call."

"Oh." Parry said. "There's another party in on it."

"No." Arbogast said. "You don't need to worry about that. It's just that I belong to an automobile club. It's not a big club but it's convenient and it has a knack of getting a line on people. So here's what I did. Now get this, and you'll see how it happens that a guy can go along for years living on breadcrumbs and out of a clear blue sky a jackpot comes along and hits him in the face. I called up this automobile club and told them a grey Pontiac convertible slammed into me and busted my car and made me a hospital case and then kept on going on a hit-run basis. I gave them the license number and I wanted to know if it was worth my while to start action. They told me to wait there and they'd call back in ten minutes. When they called back they said I should go get myself a lawyer because I really had something. They said she was a wealthy girl and they gave me her name and address. They said she was listed for a couple hundred thousand at the inside and I ought to collect plenty. You staying with me?"

"I'm right alongside you."

"That's dandy," Arbogast said. "Now stay with me while I go out of that telephone booth telling myself I'm in for a thousand or two. Or maybe four or five if I can rig up a good story. Stay with me while I walk down the street and while I pass a newsstand. Then I'm walking away from that newsstand and then I'm spinning around and running back to that newsstand and throwing two bits into the tin box and forgetting to pick up change. And there I am, looking at the front page, looking at those big black letters and looking at your face."

"You must have been glad to see me."

"Was I glad to see you? You asking me was I glad? I'm telling you I almost went into a jig. Then I pulled myself together and I started to think. What I don't understand was how she got connected with you at that particular place in the road. But I'm no dope. She must have seen you getting out of the car or else you waved to her when she passed in the Pontiac. Something like that, but I wasn't bothering myself about it. All I had to do was keep my eyes open and my head working and stay with her. So I did that. I had some money from a job I did in Sacramento and I got myself some clothes. I really splurged, because I knew I'd soon be coming into some high finance. But I didn't think in terms of a room. No, because I knew the Studebaker was going to be my home for a while, parked outside the apartment on the other side of the street. So there I am, parked there on the other side of the street and playing it conservative and taking my time. I saw her Pontiac parked outside the apartment and that was fine, but I wanted to make sure you were still with her. Late that night I saw you coming out of the apartment and that was what I'd been waiting for. I saw you getting into a taxi."

"You followed me."

"No. I'm no dope. I knew you'd come back."

"Who told you?"

"Nobody told me. Just like I say, I had my head working. That's all I need. That's why I always work alone. All I need is my head. I knew you'd come back because she was in on it with you and you had to come back sooner or later. So I stayed there and early in the morning I was there in the Studebaker and I was watching that street with both eyes. And I saw you coming down the street."

"You couldn't know it was me. My face was all bandaged."

"Look." Arbogast sounded like a patient classroom instructor. "I recognized that brand new grey suit. I checked the suit and your build and I figured it out in no time at all. You had something done to your face and that's no new story with fellows in your position.

193

I knew you were going to lamp the Studebaker and I wasn't worried about that but I didn't want you to lamp me. Not yet, anyway. So I ducked and stayed on the floor. When I got up I saw you going into the apartment house. Then I knew I had to keep you guessing, the two of you, I had to handle it like a spider, getting you in, not too fast, nothing hurried about it, just coaxing you in. I took the Studebaker down a block and parked it there so you couldn't see it from the window. And from there I watched the apartment house. And the only thing that bothered me then was maybe when you came out with your new face you wouldn't be wearing that grey suit. But I couldn't do anything about that. So I waited and then along comes another jackpot when I buy a paper from a boy and I read all about that Fellsinger job. And that doubled the pot, because now she wasn't only tied in with a jailbreak, she was connected with a murder. You see what I had on her?"

"But I didn't do it."

"I don't care whether you did it or not. The cops say you did it. That's enough for me. Anyway, I was still sort of bothered about that business of you coming out of the apartment wearing a different suit, so I decided to have a talk with you before anything like that could take place. I went up to the apartment and I rang the buzzer. That was during one of those times after she went away in the Pontiac to go shopping. You see I used to watch her going away and coming back with packages and I knew you were going to be there for a while. So there you have me ringing the buzzer and then changing my mind, saying to myself

194

to hold off for a while, play it the way I'd been playing it, taking it slow. How did I know there wasn't a third party up in that apartment? Or a fourth party? Or a mob? What I had to do was take my chances with that suit situation and wait it out until I could get you alone and away from the apartment. With all that money involved I could afford to stay in with those aces back to back and just waiting there for somebody to raise. And that raise came this morning when the grey suit came out of the apartment house. I wasn't even looking at the face. I followed the grey suit. I followed the taxi. Downtown the grey suit got out of the taxi and the whole thing was going nicely until that dick got hold of you in the diner. I saw you give him a bribe. How much did you give him?"

"Two hundred."

"You see what I'm getting at? If you could afford two hundred she must have handed you at least a couple thousand. Whoever she is, she's got feeling for you. She'll do what you say. That's why I'm arranging it the way I am. That's why we'll go there together and you'll do the asking. Now look, don't get smart."

"What's the matter?"

"You just keep your hands up, that's what's the matter. You're not dealing with no dope. I played it shrewd all the way and I aim to keep on playing it shrewd. I didn't miss a trick. I followed you from the diner and I followed you on that taxi ride to and from Golden State Park and I followed you on that department-store trip and I followed you here. At the desk I said I had a message for the man who just came in wearing a grey suit and they asked did I mean Mr.

Linnell and I said yes. That puts us here together where I wanted us to be. So now you can turn around and we'll talk it over face to face and we'll see what we got."

Parry turned and faced Arbogast and said, "You've still got that question of a third party or even a mob."

Arbogast smiled and shook his head. "You wouldn't be checking in here alone if there was a mob. You'd either want someone with you or if there was a boss the boss would want someone with you. I know how these things go. Let's call it the way it is. It's you and the girl and me and nobody else."

"I won't argue with you."

Arbogast widened the smile. "That kind of talk is music to me. Who did that job on your face?"

"I'm not saying."

"It's high-class work."

"What good is it now?"

"Don't talk like a dope," Arbogast said. "You're going to be better off now than you ever were. As soon as I get the sixty thousand I'll be clearing out and you'll be set. All right, what do you say?"

"You're holding the gun."

"Now you're using your head. I'm holding the gun. I'm holding the high cards. And as soon as I rake in the chips I walk out of the game."

"You make it sound simple."

"Sure, because that's the way it is. It's simple. Why make it complicated?"

Parry wanted to think that it was simple. He wanted to conclude that once she gave Arbogast the sixty thousand everything would be all right. And yet he knew that once Arbogast got the sixty thousand he would ask for more and keep on asking. The man was made that way. This was the first real money Arbogast had ever come up against. For Arbogast it was a delicious situation and Arbogast would want it to remain that way.

Parry told himself what he had to do. He looked at Arbogast and he told himself he had to get rid of Arbogast. He had foxed Arbogast once and maybe he could do it again.

"No," Arbogast said.

"No what?"

"Just no, that's all. The only way you get rid of me is sixty thousand. That's the only way. Look at the gun. If you try to take it I put a bullet in you. If you try to run away I put a bullet in you. And I make myself five thousand. Either way you die and either way I make money."

Parry told himself he had to get rid of Arbogast because Arbogast would keep on bothering her. Arbogast wasn't interested in him. He wished Arbogast was interested in him and only him.

Arbogast said, "All right, what do we do?"

"We'll go there," Parry said.

"That's fine," Arbogast said. "You'll stay just a bit ahead of me and you'll remember there's a gun behind you."

They walked out of the room. In the elevator Arbogast remained slightly behind Parry. In the lobby Arbogast was walking at the side of Parry and half a step behind. On the street it was the same way. The street was bright yellow from hot August sun following the heavy rain. The street was crowded with early morning activity and horns were honking and people were walking in and out of office buildings and stores.

"Let's turn here," Arbogast said.

They turned and walked up another street, then down a narrow street and Parry saw the Studebaker parked beside a two-story drygoods establishment.

"You drive," Arbogast said. He took keys out of a pocket and handed them to Parry.

Parry got in the car from the pavement side and Arbogast came sliding in beside him. Parry started the motor and sat there looking at the narrow street that went on ahead of him until it arrived at a wide and busy street.

"The whole thing won't take more than an hour," Arbogast said.

The car moved down the narrow street.

"And remember," Arbogast said, "I've got the gun right here."

"I'll remember," Parry said.

The car made a turn and it was on the wide street. Parry took it down three blocks and turned off.

"What are you doing?" Arbogast said.

"Getting out of heavy traffic," Parry said.

"Maybe that's a good idea."

"Sure it's a good idea," Parry said. "We can't afford to be stopped now. As long as we're started on this thing we might as well do it right."

The car made another turn. It was going past empty lots. There were old houses here and there. The sun was very big and very yellow and it was very hot in the car.

"I can't start worrying about her," Parry said.

"You gotta be selfish," Arbogast said. "That's the only way to get along. Even if she means something to you. Does she mean anything to you?"

"Yes."

"How bad is it?"

"It's not too bad. I'll manage to forget about her."

"That's what you gotta do," Arbogast said. "You gotta go away and forget about her. She'll be all right. I won't keep after her. Once I get that sixty thousand I'll leave her alone. You don't need to worry about anything. Hey, where we going?"

"We'll go down another few blocks and then we'll circle around and get up there from the other side of town."

The street was neglected and bumpy and the car went slowly and there were empty lots and no houses now and it was very hot and sticky and quiet except for the motor of the car.

"You do that," Arbogast said. "You go away and forget about her."

"She helped me out and I thanked her," Parry said. "I can't keep on thanking her."

"What you gotta do is get away," Arbogast said. "You got that new face and it's a dandy. All you gotta do is fix up some cards and papers for yourself and you'll be in good shape. Where do you figure on going?"

"I don't know."

"Mexico's a good bet."

"Maybe."

"You won't have any trouble in Mexico. And if you

use Arizona you won't have any trouble at the border. How much did she give you?"

"I've got about fifteen hundred left. Close to sixteen hundred."

"That's plenty. Tell you what you do. You use Arizona and when you get down there buy yourself a car in Benson. That's about thirty miles from the border. Once you got some papers arranged you won't have any trouble buying the car. They'll be only too happy to sellyou one. And once you have the car you'll have the owner's card and that's all you'll need. Do you know where you can get papers arranged?"

"I guess I can find a place."

"Sure, it's not hard. There's guys with printing presses who specialize in that sort of thing. Once you get to Benson and buy that car you'll be all right."

"They'll ask questions at the border."

"Sure they'll ask questions. Don't you know how to answer questions?"

"They'll ask me why I'm going to Mexico."

"And you'll tell them you're going there to mine silver. Or you're going there to look for oil. Or you just want a vacation. It don't make any difference what you tell them. All you gotta do is talk easy and don't worry about anything and don't get yourself mixed up. Didn't you learn all these things when you were in Quentin?"

"I didn't mix much in Quentin."

"You should of mixed. It's always a good idea to mix. That's the only way to learn things. Especially in a place like Quentin. And you don't need to tell me anything about Quentin. They put me in there twice.

And I learned things I never knew before. I learned tricks that got me out of more jams than I can count. You got some shrewd boys in Quentin."

"Where can I get the papers arranged?"

"Well," Arbogast said. "Let's see now. There's a guy I know in Sacramento but that won't do because you'd have to give my name and I can't act loose in Sacramento for a while yet. Then there's a guy in Nevada, in Carson City, but I did a job in Carson City a few weeks ago so I'm still hot there so that lets Carson City out. So let's see, now. Las Vegas is out because I'm wanted there and let's see, maybe if we come back to California, but, no, I'm still hot in Stockton and Modesto and Visalia, it was all little jobs but these small town police are terriers, that's exactly what they are. And don't go thinking they're dumb, because they're anything but dumb. Don't go calling them dopes. Especially in some of these little California towns. I tell you California is plenty mean and the sooner I get out when I get the cash—"

"Get what cash?"

"The two hundred thousand, I mean the sixty."

"You mean the sixty thousand dollars."

"Sure, that's what I mean. The sixty. What did you think I meant?"

The car was going very slowly now and the lots were very empty. There was thin wooded area going away from the lots on the left and on the right the nearest houses were away past low hills and almost at the horizon. In front the bumpy road was all yellow dirt going ahead slowly as the car went slowly, going ahead toward more stretches of empty lots. The sun was banging away a hard and bright yellow steadiness that seemed to splash and throw itself around, thick and wriggling and squirming in its hot stickiness.

"I figured you meant the sixty," Parry said. "We'll turn soon. There's an intersection down ahead."

The car crawled. Under the hot sun the empty lots were very bright and yellow and quiet. The grinding motor was a sphere of sound complete in itself and apart from the quiet of the empty lots.

"Where's that intersection you were talking about?"

"We'll come to it." He wondered how long he could stretch this out.

"I don't see anything out there," Arbogast said.

"It's there," Parry said. He half-turned and saw Arbogast sitting beside him, leaning forward and looking ahead and trying to see an intersection. Then Arbogast was looking at him and waiting for him to say something and he said, "I wish you could think of a place."

"What kind of a place?"

"A place where I could get those papers arranged."

"Yeah," Arbogast said. "That's something you'll need to do. You can't overlook that. You'll need papers and cards. Let's see now, let's see if I can help you out. You'll be going through Nevada by train or maybe bus is better. Yeah, that's what you better do. You better use one of those two-by-four bus companies. Let's see if I can think of a place. You can't do anything in California and I can't think of any place in Nevada. Let's see, you'll be buying that car in Arizona, in Benson, so let's see what's north of Benson. Yeah, there's a place. There's a guy I know in

202

Maricopa."

"Maricopa?"

"Yeah. You ever been there?"

"I was born and raised there."

"Come to think of it, you did tell me. Yeah, that day I picked you up you said Maricopa when I asked you where you came from. It's funny, aint it?"

"It's one of those things."

"It just goes to show you we're always going back. You went away from Maricopa and now you gotta go back there. How long since you left there?"

"About seventeen years."

"And now you're going back. Out of all the places you could go it's gotta be Maricopa. That's really something."

"Who do I see?"

"Well, this printer I know. He did a few license jobs for me and some guys I sent to him. He knows his work and he's tight as a rivet. He'll remember my name. It's been more than a year now but he'll remember. He'll give you what you want and he'll take your money and that's as far as it goes. You look him up when you get to Maricopa. His name's Ferris."

"What?"

"Tom Ferris."

"That name's familiar," Parry said.

"What?"

"That's right," Parry said. "Tom Ferris, the printer. I remember him."

Arbogast slapped a hand on a knee. "Now what do you think of that?" he said. "You know him. That takes it. I tell you, that takes it. You're gonna go back to Maricopa and you're gonna see your old friend Ferris. Good old Ferris is gonna fix up those papers for you. Well, I'll tell you something. That takes it."

"Tom Ferris." Parry smiled. He shook his head slowly.

"And he prints fake cards and papers for guys on the run," Arbogast said. "He prints the town paper and people think he's as straight as they come. You'd never believe it, would you?"

Parry stopped smiling. He said, "How do I work it?"

"It's easy," Arbogast said. "You just go there and look him up. Get him alone and tell him Arbogast sent you. Tell him what you want and the price you're willing to pay. That's all he wants to know. It's gonna cost you about three hundred for a license and a few other cards and papers that you'll need to have. He knows all about it. He knows just what you need. He's been doing this work for years."

"How long will it take?"

"Maybe an hour. He'll go to work right away. You can't tell me it aint worth a few hundred."

"It's worth every cent of that," Parry said.

"Sure. Well, I'm telling you, that takes it. Now where's that intersection?"

"Right up ahead."

"I don't see it."

"It's there."

"I tell you I don't see it," Arbogast said. "There's no intersection. What are you trying to pull?"

"We've got to stay away from traffic."

"That don't mean we gotta go to the South Pole.

204

I'm telling you there's no intersection up ahead."

"I'm telling you there is." He brought the car to a stop, readied himself.

"And I say no," Arbogast said. "And I've got the gun. Look. Go on, look at it."

"All right," Parry said, "it's your car. It's your gun." He reached forward to release the emergency brake and then without touching the emergency brake, he sent his hands toward the wrist of the hand that held the gun. Arbogast was raising the gun to fire but Parry had hold of the wrist and was twisting it. Arbogast wouldn't let go of the gun and Parry kept twisting and Arbogast let out a yell. And Parry kept twisting and Arbogast let out another yell and then he dropped the gun and it fell on the space of empty seat between Parry and Arbogast. With his free hand Arbogast grabbed at the gun and Parry kept twisting the wrist of the other hand and Arbogast's head went back and he yelled and kept on yelling and forgot about taking the gun. Parry released Arbogast's wrists and snatched at the gun and took it. He got his finger against the trigger and he pointed the gun at Arbogast's face.

CHAPTER 17

Arbogast looked at the gun. He started to go back. He kept going back until he came against the door and then he tried to push himself through the door.

"Just stay where you are," Parry said.

"Don't shoot me in the face," Arbogast said.

Parry lowered the gun and had it aimed at Arbogast's chest.

"How's that?" Parry said.

"Look," Arbogast said. "Let me go now and I promise you I'll keep on going and I'll never bother you again."

Parry shook his head.

"Please," Arbogast said.

Parry shook his head.

"I had an idea you were going to pull something like this," Arbogast said.

"Why didn't you do something about it?" Parry asked.

"Why did I have to start with you in the first

206

place?" Arbogast said.

"I can answer that," Parry said. "You're a crook."

"There's honor among crooks," Arbogast said. "Believe me, there is. And if I give you my word I'll go away and won't bother you—"

Parry shook his head.

"Are you going to shoot me?" Arbogast said.

Parry shook his head.

"What are you going to do?" Arbogast said.

Parry gazed past Arbogast's head. He saw the stretch of empty lot very yellow under the bright yellow sky and beyond the lot the beginnings of woodland. He said, "Get out of the car."

"What are you doing to do with me?"

"Open the door and get out," Parry said.

"Please—"

"Do as I tell you or I'll be forced to shoot you."

Arbogast opened the door. As he stood there on the side of the road he looked up and down and he saw nothing but emptiness. Then Parry was turning off the motor and coming out there with him and closing the door. And they stood out there together and Parry had the gun pointed at Arbogast's chest.

"Let's take a stroll," Parry said.

"Where are we going?"

"Into the woods."

"Why?"

"I want us to be alone. I don't want any interference."

"You're going to shoot me," Arbogast said.

"I won't shoot you unless you make a try for the gun," Parry said.

They were walking across the empty lot, and Parry

had the gun aimed at Arbogast's ribs.

They weren't saying anything as they walked across the lot. Then they were past the lot and they were going through the woods. It was moist in the woods, very sticky and very hot. They were going slowly.

They went about seventy yards into the woods and then Parry said, "I guess this is all right."

Arbogast turned and looked at the gun.

Parry looked at the place on Arbogast's middle where the gun was aiming. Parry said, "Did you kill Fellsinger?"

"No."

"Did you follow me to Fellsinger's apartment?"

"No."

"But you knew Irene Janney had money. You knew she had two hundred thousand dollars."

"Yes, I knew that. I told you."

"And you wanted to get your hands on that cash."

"I'll admit that."

"All right then, it checks. Part of it, anyway. Two hundred thousand is something out of the ordinary. You could have figured it this way—you could have said to yourself she'd get a year or two for helping me get away. But if I killed somebody while I was loose then she'd be in real trouble and she'd get maybe ten years or even twenty. And you had your mind set on that two hundred thousand. So maybe you followed the taxi when I left her apartment."

"No."

"Maybe you followed the taxi and when I went in there you followed me and you were hiding in the vestibule and watching to see what button I pressed. Then after I left you pressed that same button. And

208

here's what you could have been thinking—that the taxi driver would be a witness. At least when the police gave him my description he'd say I was the man who came to the apartment house at a certain hour that night. So the taxi driver would be one thing and my fingerprints here and there would be another. You knew I wasn't going up there to kill Fellsinger and you knew I was going up there to see somebody who would help me. You didn't know it was Fellsinger but you knew it was a friend of mine. And you knew the police would tie me in and when they got my fingerprints and when they got a statement from the taxi driver they would come right out and say I did it. You knew all that. So maybe you went up there and killed Fellsinger."

"No."

"It's got to be. You admit you were watching her apartment house. You admit you were waiting for me to come out. That checks. You had your car there. And that checks. And you could have followed me to Fellsinger's apartment. And you had a reason for killing Fellsinger. Because you knew I'd be blamed and that would bring her in on it. So that checks."

"No," Arbogast said. "I didn't kill Fellsinger."

"Then who did? Somebody did, and it wasn't me. So who was it if it wasn't you?"

"I don't know."

"Whoever killed Fellsinger followed me there, went up and killed him after I went away. I know that much. So let's go back. You were outside her apartment house. You saw me get in a taxi. You saw the taxi going down the street. Did the taxi pass you?"

"Yes."

209

"Did you follow the taxi?"

"No. I told you no."

"You just stayed there and watched the taxi going away?"

"That's right."

"You're a liar. I walked three blocks before I got in that taxi."

"And I followed you for three blocks," Arbogast said.

"You said you stayed there."

"I said I stayed at the place where I saw you getting in the taxi. That was as far as I wanted to go. Look, here's what I did. I saw you walking down the street. You made about a block, and then I put the car in gear and followed you. I stayed about half a block behind you and I had the car in second and I was just creeping along and watching you. Then you were about three blocks away from the apartment house and you were getting in that taxi."

"What did you do?"

"I pulled up at the curb."

"And then what did you do?"

"I stayed there. I watched you going away in the taxi."

"And then what?"

"I made a turn and went back to the apartment house. I parked on the other side of the street, far down the block."

"You say you made a turn. What kind of a turn? Around the corner?"

"No," Arbogast said. "It was a U-turn."

Parry examined Arbogast's eyes. Parry said, "You're sure it was a U-turn?"

"I'm giving it to you straight. I made that U-turn and went back and parked across the street from the apartment house. I knew you'd come back."

"How did you know?"

"I'm no dope. You had a perfect set-up there. You get new clothes out of it, and I knew you were getting money out of it. And when they gave me the lowdown on her they told me she was single and that meant you were alone with her up there so it was perfect for you and you'd be a dope to walk out on it. What I figured was you'd stay there until things calmed down and then you'd make a break out of town."

"Now you're sure you made a U-turn? You're sure you didn't go around the corner and up the next block and then down?"

"Look," Arbogast said. "If I made a turn around the corner and up the next block and then down it would've brought me on the same side of the street as the apartment house. You lamped the car, didn't you?"

"Yes."

"You saw it was on the other side of the street?"

"Yes," Parry said.

"The front of the car was facing you, wasn't it?"

"Yes."

"All right, that proves I made a U-turn. And what's all this about a U-turn?"

"Two U-turns."

"Well, sure it was two U-turns," Arbogast said. "I was parked on the other side of the street when I saw you coming out of the apartment house. I had to make a U-turn to follow you, didn't I? And I had to make another U-turn to come back."

211

"You made the first U-turn right away?"

"No," Arbogast said. "I told you I waited until you were about a block away."

"You had your headlights off?"

"They were off. I'm not a dope."

"That second U-turn. Tell me about it."

"What's there to tell about a U-turn? You turn the steering wheel and you turn the car around and that's all there is to it."

"That second U-turn. Did you make it right away?"

"No. Like I told you I stayed there and watched the taxi going away."

"You're trying to tell me you saw the taxi going away and you just stayed there and watched it go away. That doesn't make sense."

"My car can't do more than thirty."

"All right, that does make sense," Parry said. "But you didn't know the taxi would go past thirty. So again it doesn't make sense. There was a reason why you didn't follow that taxi and I know what it is and you know I know what it is. You saw a car going after that taxi."

"What do you mean a car?"

"A car. A machine. An automobile. You saw it following the taxi. That's why you waited there. You saw that car going down the street with its headlights turned off. You didn't know who it was but you knew it was going after the taxi. So here's what you thought. You thought it could be the police. Then again maybe it wasn't the police. And as long as you weren't sure you decided to make a U-turn and go back and watch the apartment house and wait for me. You figured maybe the taxi would shake the car and maybe I'd come back and even if I didn't come back there was a chance I'd stay on the loose. And even though I was on the loose you had something on her. And as long as you had something on her you were going to stay in the neighborhood and watch the apartment house. So that night you were playing for say ten or fifteen thousand. The next morning when you saw me coming back with the bandages on my face you knew you were still in it for ten or fifteen. Later that day you were patting yourself on the back and saying I'm no dope because a morning paper told you of a man murdered the night before and the police said I did it. So then you knew you were in it for all she had. You saw yourself with every cent of her two hundred thousand. Now all you see is a gun. And all you know is you've got to tell me about that car."

"I didn't see any car."

"Tell me or I'll shoot you above the knee. I'll keep on shooting until I tear your leg off."

"There wasn't any car," Arbogast said.

"There had to be a car. And it had to be a certain kind of a car. You got a chance to walk away from here with both legs if you tell me what kind of car it was and if it's the same car I'm thinking of."

Arbogast looked at Parry's face.

Parry stood there waiting. He knew he had thrown everything into that one. That was the big one. That was the big bluff.

Arbogast looked at the gun.

"I don't have a thing to lose," Parry said.

Arbogast took a lot of air in his mouth and swallowed it.

"I can see it's no use," Parry said. "You won't tell me. And if you do tell me you won't be telling the truth. You've tried to make things miserable for her and for me and now I'm going to make things miserable for you."

"I'll tell you," Arbogast said.

"Tell me and make it good the first time, because there won't be a second time."

"It was a roadster," Arbogast said. "It had a canvas top and it was a bright color. I think it was orange."

"Bright orange," Parry said.

"A bright orange roadster," Arbogast said.

"And who was in it?"

"I couldn't see."

"All right," Parry said. "I guess that doesn't matter. I guess I got everything I need now."

"What happens to me?"

"That's not my worry."

"What are you going to do with me?"

"Nothing. I'm going to leave you here. What do I need you for? You're out of it now."

"If I'm out of it, let me go."

"Sure," Parry said. "You can go. Just turn around and start walking."

"Let me take my car."

"No," Parry said. "I'm taking that."

"You can't take my car."

"And you didn't think I could take your gun either but I took it."

"You won't get away."

"I'm not trying to get away," Parry said. "Not any more. I've got the big lead now. You handed it to me on a silver platter. You followed me and kept on following me until finally you gave me exactly what I needed. Maybe that's the way things are arranged. I don't know, do you?"

"I'm not out of it yet," Arbogast said.

"Maybe it's got to be that things always turn out this way," Parry said. "Maybe there's a certain arrangement to things and even if it takes a long time it finally has to work itself out."

"You're not taking that car."

"You can't tell me what I can take and what I can't take. All you can do is stand there and tell yourself you've lost a couple hundred thousand dollars. You know it's wonderful when guys like you lose out. It makes guys like me believe maybe we got a chance in this world."

"I tell you I'm not out of it yet."

"Take a walk, mister. Turn around and take a walk."

"I'm not through yet," Arbogast said. "I started out to get something and I'm gonna get it."

And he came leaping at Parry. And Parry lifted the gun and fired in the air hoping to scare Arbogast but Arbogast was beyond scaring and came slamming into Parry and they went down together with Arbogast trying for the gun. Parry stretched his arm back to get the gun away from Arbogast's hand. The weight of Arbogast was heavy on Parry and Arbogast went sliding forward to get the gun and Parry tried to slide away and Arbogast kept on sliding forward. Parry twisted and rolled but Arbogast was there now with the gun and trying with both hands to get the gun out of Parry's hand. Parry held onto the gun. Arbogast used his knees to keep Parry down and he was still going forward and making noises down in his throat

215

as he tried to get the gun out of Parry's hand. Parry wouldn't let go of the gun and Arbogast kept going forward until he got a knee against Parry's throat and when he knew he had the knee there he pressed with the knee. Parry's head went back as the knee went jamming against his throat and hurting and blocking the air and the knee pressed harder and already it was bad and then it was very bad and it was getting worse but he wouldn't let go of the gun. And he had a feeling that his hand had become part of the gun and it was impossible for anything to get the gun away from his hand and he had a feeling that Arbogast knew that also because now the knee was taking everything away from him because the knee was so heavy and fierce against his throat and taking everything away from him and now the pain in his throat was a long tube of pain that went out from both ends, went up to his eyes and down to his stomach and twirled itself and kept twirling as the knee pressed harder. And he wouldn't let go of the gun as the pain went driving into him and going up and down the tube and in his stomach the tube was glossy and purple and in his brain the tube was black and burning and somewhere in the middle the tube was clear and it was a glass tube and he could see into it and know that Arbogast was no longer trying hard for the gun but trying hard to kill him with the knee in the throat. He could see it in the glassy clear middle of the tube, Arbogast burying him here and then going back to her and getting sixty thousand from her and going away and getting twenty more thousand from her and going away and coming back and getting thirty more thousand, forty more thousand, going away, coming back, going away and coming back and he could see her giving the money to Arbogast and he could get the sound of her asking Arbogast where he was and what had happened to him and Arbogast telling her he was somewhere around and what difference did it make where he was and what he was doing as long as she gave the money when she was asked for it. And the pain came slashing into his throat and pouring into the tube, going up and down, going fast now and it was killing him. Outside the pain he felt something on his hand, like a little warm breeze warmer than the warm yellow air, and he knew it was the breath of Arbogast, coming from the face of Arbogast close to his hand as Arbogast kept jamming the knee into his throat. He twisted his hand and, bringing it up as he twisted it, bringing the gun up, far outside the tube of pain he heard the scream of Arbogast and then he pulled the trigger.

CHAPTER 18

All of the tube was black and it was thick now, filling his throat, and in his head it was a big ball of black nothing. He could feel it up there and he knew it was getting bigger and he wondered if it was going to get too big. He could hear the sound of his dragging breath, and it was as if his breath was cinders grinding across more cinders.

Then it began to go away, the black and the cinders. He had his eyes closed as he reached up and loosened his tie and unbuttoned his collar. Now the air was going in smoother and faster and the tube was getting thin and then it was melting and then it was gone.

He opened his eyes. He saw dark brown branches and bright green leaves against the heavy hot yellow. He closed his eyes and told himself it would be nice to sleep for a while.

Gliding into sleep was very nice, and staying in sleep was soft and light and proper, because it was not a full sleep and he sensed the comfort of it as he rested there with his eyes closed, taking in the air and getting rid of the shock and the hurt.

Then when he opened his eyes again he knew he had slept there for a couple of hours at least and he knew he was much better now and he could get up. He got up slowly. He wondered if he could stand without leaning against anything. He could stand all right. He could move his legs. He felt his throat and it seemed to feel swollen but there was no pain now, only a heaviness on the outside. He turned and looked at Arbogast.

He saw Arbogast resting face down. The back of the head bulged out.

He went over and rolled the body face up. He looked at the face.

The eyes were open and wrenched loose, and there was blood where the flesh was split. The nose was torn apart and the hole was big and black and green and yellow, going up and going deep and going through the head and making the bulge. There was blood all over the mouth and all over the chin. There was dried blood in the ears and clotted blood on the coat and the shirtfront.

There was blood all over the gun where it rested near the body.

Without sound the body said, "I started out to get something."

Without sound Parry said, "You got it."

He stooped to pick up the gun and he saw the

219

sticky blood all over his hand. He took out a handkerchief and wiped off the blood. Then he examined himself for more blood. He couldn't see any blood on his clothing and he knew the body had fallen away from him when the bullet went in.

He picked up the gun, keeping the handkerchief between his hand and the gun so as not to stain his hand with more blood. Then he walked deeper into the woods and established a hole for the gun. He covered the hole and smoothed it carefully. Then he walked away several yards, made another hole and buried the blood-stained handkerchief. Then he came back to the body and looked at it.

Without thinking of it, he reached in a coat pocket, took out a pack of cigarettes and a book of matches. He put a cigarette in his mouth as he looked at the body. Standing there and looking at the body he lit the cigarette.

He stood there smoking the cigarette and looking at the body.

He was puzzled.

He couldn't understand why he felt no regret, why he felt no horror at the sight of this dead thing on the ground, this thing he had killed. It had always seemed impossible that he would ever kill anyone, that he would ever have either the cause or the impulse.

Wondering about it, he knew he wasn't glad. At the same time he wasn't sorry. It was something mechanical and as he stood there looking at the body he knew it was one of those logical patterns. It was geometry. He was alive and the thing on the ground was dead. It had to be that way and the pattern was expanding now, taking in Irene, because he knew now he had wanted to stay with Irene, and he knew now every time he had gone away from her he had wanted to go back. And each time he had managed to hurdle that want as it came rolling toward him. Now it was with him again, greater than ever before, and there was no need for hurdling it, because he knew the identity of the murderer. He knew how and why Gert and Fellsinger had been killed, and he knew what he had to do now. He was building the method, telling himself how he could prove the guilt of the other person, forcing the showdown that would display and clarify his own innocence. And the pattern kept expanding, showing him the simple and ordinary happiness he had always wanted, the happiness he had expected to find with Gert, the clean and decent happiness of a little guy who wasn't important and had no special urge to be important and wanted nothing more than a daily job to do and someone to open a door for him at night and give him a smile.

It kept expanding. It began to glow. He would get a confession from the murderer after showing the murderer the absence of any loophole. And then his girl would be waiting for him. He had tears in his eyes, knowing she was waiting for him even now, knowing she wouldn't need to wait much longer. The happiness flowed from the pattern and flowed over him. A job in a war plant, and Sundays with his girl, and every morning and every night with his girl, his little girl.

He was telling himself that everything was all right

now.

He walked away from the body. He walked through the woods, came out on the empty lot, walking slowly. He walked across the empty lot, slowly working on the cigarette as he told himself what he had to do. He crossed the road and got in the car and turned on the motor. Before he released the brake he turned his head and looked across the empty lot, across the yellow emptiness broken by the line of green woodland. And the woodland seemed very quiet and passive.

Then the car was moving. He took it into a U-turn and started back toward the city. His wrist watch was still working and it showed him two forty-five.

Coming into the city he parked the car on a narrow side street three blocks away from a busy section. He was feeling hungry and the pain of his throat had gone away completely. He told himself there was no reason why he shouldn't eat something. He got out of the car and walked toward the busy section. Then he was in a restaurant and he had pork chops and vegetables, a cup of coffee and a piece of pie. He sat there with another cup of coffee and a cigarette. He had another cigarette and then he walked out of the restaurant and went down the street and stood on a corner waiting for a taxi. Three taxis went past without paying any attention to him. The fourth taxi picked him up.

The taxi moved slowly through heavy traffic.

Parry looked at his trousers, his sleeves. He looked all over and there was no blood. The taxi was making a turn. He lit another cigarette. The taxi was getting away from the center of town. He moved across the seat so he could see himself in the rearview mirror. He arranged his tie and smoothed his hair. He leaned back and breathed the heat that gushed in through open windows. The taxi made another turn. It was going faster now.

The taxi went up a steep street, then down, then up again. Then the taxi was going through a section devoted to apartment houses. The taxi came to a light and stopped and there was a drugstore on the corner.

"I'll get out here," Parry said.

"You said—"

"I know, but I'll get out here. It's only a couple blocks away."

"You're the doctor."

Parry paid his fare and walked into the drugstore. He picked up a telephone book and his forefinger ran down a line of names. He closed the book, went over to the counter and made change, getting two dimes and a nickel for a quarter. He went into a telephone booth and dialed a number.

Someone said, "Hello."

"Mrs. Rapf?"

"Yes?"

"How are you, Madge?"

"Who is this?"

"A friend of your husband."

"I don't have a husband. Anyway, I don't live with him."

"I know, that's why I'm calling."

"What do you want?"

"I'd like to meet you."

"Say, what is this?"

"Nothing very special, except I just started working here a few weeks ago and I don't know many people. I met your husband and he told me about you. He gave you a nice build-up."

"Oh, he did, did he? What are you, a leper or something?"

"I told him I'd like to meet you and he gave me your number. I hope you don't mind."

"I think you got a lot of crust."

"May I see you?"

"You may not."

"Look, Madge, I think you'd like me."

"Who gave you permission to call me Madge?"

"When you see me you'll give me permission."

"Oh, I will, will I?"

"I think so. From what your husband said, I think you're the type I like. And I'm sure I'm the type you like."

"I don't like the fresh type."

"I'm not really fresh. Just sort of informal."

"What do you look like?"

"I'm good looking."

"How tall are you?"

"Average."

"Thin?"

"Yes."

"How old are you?"

"Thirty-six."

"How come you're not married?"

"I was. Twice. They weren't the type I was looking

for. I'm looking for a certain type."

"You don't mince words, do you?"

"What's the use of mincing words?"

"What's your name?"

"Allan."

"Allan what?"

"Just call me Allan."

"What did my husband say?"

"I'll tell you when I see you."

"How do you know you're going to see me?"

"I don't know, because that's up to you. But if you're at all curious, I'm right here in the neighborhood. I could drop in and say hello. When we see each other we'll know if it's worthwhile getting started. And if it is we'll have dinner tonight."

"I'd like to know what he said."

"I'll tell you."

"Tell me now."

"I'd like to, but that might spoil my chances of seeing you."

"You putting a sword over my head?"

"Not because I want to. But I'm very anxious to meet you."

"I'm not dressed. I was in the bathtub. It's such a hot day."

"There's no hurry."

"I'll tell you what. I'll slip something on. Be here in fifteen minutes, make it twenty."

"All right, twenty minutes," he said, and he hung up. He walked out of the booth and went over to the counter and asked a clerk for a pack of cigarettes and the clerk handed them to him. Then he glanced at his wrist watch. The clerk asked him if there was anything else. He said he didn't think so. Then he saw boxes of candy stacked in pyramid fashion and he asked the price and the clerk said two dollars and he asked the clerk if there was something more expensive. The clerk ducked under the counter and came up with a violet box with violet satin ribbons all around it and said four and a half. Parry said that was really expensive and it ought to be something special. The clerk said it was really something special, all right, it was continental style chocolates and there wasn't much of that stuff around any more and this was the last box in the store and if he wanted something really special he ought to take this while the taking was good. He bought the box for four dollars and fifty cents plus tax and he told the clerk to wrap it up fancy and the clerk smiled knowingly and went to work on the box. Parry took the package and walked over to the magazine stand and stood there looking at the covers. A woman came in and bought a hot-water bottle. A little boy came in and bought a bar of candy. A man came in holding a hand to a swollen jaw with a prescription in the other hand. Parry glanced at his wrist watch. A young woman came in and asked for something and the clerk tried to make a date with her and she asked the clerk why wasn't he wearing a discharge pin. He said he had a double hernia and he'd show her if she wanted to see and she walked out. The clerk came out from behind the counter and came over to Parry and said things like that burned him up. He opened his shirt and showed Parry an awful looking scar that

226

ran from his chest down along his ribs and he said he got that at Kasserine Pass. Parry glanced at his wrist watch. The clerk said it burned him up the way people went around making remarks and he said he was good and fed up with people anyway. He was buttoning his shirt and saying one of these fine days he was going to haul off and punch somebody in the mouth. The owner of the store came out a small side room and stood in the center of the store looking out through the open doorway at the black street turned yellow by the sun. A little girl came in and said she forgot what her mother sent her for and went out again. The owner of the store put his hand in front of an electric fan and shook his head and walked across the store and turned on another electric fan. A sailor came in and sat down at the soda fountain and asked for a peach ice-cream soda. The clerk said there wasn't any peach. The sailor took strawberry and sat there mixing the ice cream with the soda and said that was the only way to enjoy an ice-cream soda. An old woman came in and bought a bottle of mineral oil and walked out. The sailor said it was sure a hot day and the clerk said it sure was and the sailor asked for another strawberry ice-cream soda. Parry glanced at his wrist watch and walked out of the store.

He walked down the street, turned, went down another street, turned and he was on the street that was all apartment houses. He knew the street. He knew the apartment house, the white brick structure with the black iron gate and the black window frames. He lit a cigarette, crossed the street and went through the open gate. He glanced at his wrist watch as he entered the vestibule. Then he looked at the listing and he saw her name and he pressed the button. There was a buzzing response. He opened the door and went into the lobby.

In the elevator he dropped the cigarette and stepped on it. The elevator took him to the fifth floor. He walked down the hall. He remembered the hall, everything about it. He told himself there was a certain way he had to go about this, and what he ought to do was stand here a moment and itemize the things he had to say and the order in which they were to be said. Then he was thinking that it might not be a good idea to rehearse it this way because that would be mechanical and he had to avoid the mechanical now. He remembered the way he had pulled it out of Arbogast, the way he had hammered away at the U-turns to get Arbogast's mind back to that night and specific moments of that night, getting Arbogast to see it again, going back to the first U-turn, the waiting before the first U-turn, the waiting before the second U-turn, seeing that Arbogast wasn't really back there yet and drilling the U-turns into Arbogast, keeping Arbogast there with the U-turns, keeping Arbogast on that street in those moments, then the first U-turn, and then the second U-turn, and the interval again between the first and second U-turn so that Arbogast would stay there and be there long enough to remember. He had not planned that and he knew that if he had planned something it would not have been the U-turns. And it was only because of the U-turns that he had managed to get it out of Arbogast. It was a spontaneous maneuver and there was nothing mechanical in it and there must be nothing mechanical in this.

He was at the door now.

He knocked on the door.

CHAPTER 19

The door opened.

She stood there looking at his face. Then she was looking him up and down. Then again she was looking at his face.

She was thin. She was about five feet four and she didn't weigh much more than a hundred.

She had an ordinary face without anything pretty in it. She had eyes the color of an old telegraph pole. Her nose was short and wide at the base and too wide for her face and her mouth was too large. But she wasn't really ugly. It was just that she wasn't pretty. She was tan and there was something artificial about the tan, as if she got it from some kind of a lamp. Her hair was dyed darkish orange. She wore it parted in the center and brought back with her ears showing. She was wearing a bright orange house coat and pale orange slacks and she wore sandals that showed her toenails painted bright orange. She had a cigarette in her hand and the smoke came up and rolled slowly over her head.

"Come in," she said.

Parry walked in and closed the door. He stood on a dark orange broadloom carpet. It was fairly new. Everything in the apartment was changed and fairly new. Everything was orange or leaned toward orange. There were orange lines running down and crossways on the frames of the big window. There was a big vase of glazed orange on the left side of the window and on the right side there was a conference of Indian pottery all white except for zigzag orange lines around the middle.

She seated herself in a low and rounded chair of pale orange and indicated the dark orange sofa.

Parry sat down. He was looking at her. He put the package on the sofa.

She said, "I don't think I should have let you come here."

"Don't you like what you see?"

"That's not the point. I don't usually do things this way."

"Well, I'm glad I came."

"Would you like a drink?" She was looking at the package.

"Please. Something cold."

She got up and went into the kitchen. She came out with a tray that had two tall glasses half-filled with ice, a dish of sliced limes and a bottle of carbonated water. She opened a pale orange cabinet and took out a bottle of gin. She mixed the drinks.

Parry sipped his drink and looked at the carpet.

She said, "What did my husband say?" She glanced at the package.

Parry looked up. She was opening her mouth to get at the drink. He saw gold inlays glimmering among her teeth.

He said, "Gave me a description."

"Accurate?"

"Yes."

She took a big drink. "What else?" She glanced again at the package.

"He said you weren't easy to get along with."

"Maybe I'm not."

"Maybe that's what I like."

"Are you easy to get along with?"

"Sometimes. It depends."

She smiled at him. Her mouth was open and he saw the gold inlays again. She said, "What else?"

"About me?"

"No. What my husband said about me." She looked at the package.

"He said you almost drove him out of his mind."

"And what else?" She had her mouth open wide as she smiled.

He look at the gold inlays. He said, "Well, your husband claimed you had a habit of putting on the act."

"What kind of an act?"

"Acting as if you didn't have much brains, merely an ignorant sort of pest."

"Is that what he really said?"

"Yes, and he said you were really a shrewd manipulator and when you were out to get something you stopped at nothing. He said he left you because he was afraid of you."

"And what do you think?"

"I think he had something there."

"Do you think you'd be afraid of me?" She looked at the package.

"Every now and then. And that's where you'd have a problem. You'd have to guess when."

She laughed. The gold inlays caught some of the sun and juggled it. She said, "What do you do?" And she laughed again.

"I work in an investment security house."

She stopped laughing. She looked at him. She said, "What do you do there?"

"I'm a customer's man."

"What house?"

"Kinney."

"How long have you worked there?"

"Only a few weeks. I told you I just got in town."

"How did you meet my husband?"

"He came in to make an investment."

"Where's he getting the money to make investments?"

"He didn't invest much."

"How much?"

"I'm not saying."

She stood up. She said, "Are you going to tell me?"

"No."

"All right then, get out of here."

"Okay." He got up and he was going toward the

233

door.

She started to laugh. He turned and looked at her. The gold inlays seemed magnified. She said, "You were really going to go, weren't you?"

"Yes."

"And would you have gotten in touch with me again?"

"No."

"Why not?" She looked at the package on the sofa.

"You'd start asking questions about him. You've got him on your mind."

"Don't be silly."

"All right, then, you've got his money on your mind."

"You don't go for that, do you?"

"Part of it I don't go for. I don't care what you've got on your mind. But when I'm around I don't want to hear questions about him or his money."

"Who said you were going to be around?"

"I didn't. Neither did you. But we both know."

"Don't tell me what I know." She looked at the package.

"All right, I won't. There's no point in my telling you if you know already."

She looked at the package. She said, "Is that for me?"

"Yes."

She went over and opened the package. She untied the violet satin ribbons and opened the box and looked at the chocolate candy.

She smiled. She was very pleased. She said, "This is lovely."

234

"I'm glad you like it."

She put a piece of chocolate in her mouth and he saw the gold inlays again. She munched the chocolate and said, "It's very delicious."

She sat down in the low rounded chair with the box of candy in her lap. Her mouth was soft with contentment and her eyes glittered with anticipation. She was stimulated now and that was what he wanted to see.

She said, "Thank you for the candy, Allan. Allan what?"

"Linnell."

She was looking at his mouth. She said, "When I looked at the candy I knew I was going to like the taste of it." She kept on looking at his mouth.

He said, "Well what do you think? Do you think we've got something here?"

She leaned back and lifted another piece of candy. She smiled and said, "Allan Linnell." Then she put the candy in her mouth and bit into it.

And that told him he was ready.

He said, "I should have brought the candy in an orange box."

She watched him gazing at the dark orange carpet. She said, "Yes, it's my big weakness."

"I bet everything you own is on the orange side."

"Just about." She was looking at his mouth.

"Even your car?"

"Even my car. It's bright orange. And my jewelry is orange beryl. And my favorite drink is an orange blossom, just because of the color."

"Yes," he said. "I guess certain colors appeal to

235

certain people."

She was looking at his mouth as he said that, and when it got through her ears and into her head her gaze dropped and she was looking at his suit. Then her eyes came up again and she was looking at his eyes. Then her gaze dropped once more and she was looking at the grey worsted fabric and the violet stripe. And she looked at the violet box of candy. And she looked at the violet lines in the grey suit. And she looked at his eyes.

Then she shuddered and closed her eyes.

Then she opened her eyes and looked at him.

Without moving from the chair she was trying to take herself out of the room.

He said, "You know. You recognize the suit. You got a good look at it that night. Now you're looking at my face and you don't believe it but there's nothing else for you to do and no other way for you to take it. You've got to believe it."

She was trying to get out of the chair and she couldn't move.

He said, "It's really me."

"Go away," she said. "Go away and leave me alone."

"I can't do that, Madge. I can't do that now. I'm the Pest now. You've always been the Pest but now I'm the Pest. I've got to be. It's this way, Madge, I've got to stay here with you and I've got to pester you because I know you killed Gert and you killed Fellsinger and I've got to make you own up to it."

"Go away."

"You can't send me away, Madge. You did that

once but you can't do it now. You're very clever, Madge, but you're not an enchantress. In a dream I had you were a bright orange enchantress on a high trapeze, and you got me to go up there with you on the trapeze, and once you had me up there you let me drop. I was broken and dying and everyone was sorry for me. And you were up there on the high trapeze, laughing at me and showing your gold inlays. But I got away from the dream. And you can't get away. You're still up there on the high trapeze and you're all alone."

"Go away, Vincent. Please go away. If you go away now they'll never find you."

"Now I want them to find me."

"They'll kill you."

"Do I look worried?"

She shuddered again. She stared at him.

He said, "No, Madge, I'm not worried. I know you did it and I know I can convince them you did it. I've got facts to prove you followed me from Irene Janney's apartment the night Fellsinger was murdered. That's the first thing I'm going to give them. Then I'll take them back to the day you killed Gert. I'll tell them why you killed her and I'll show them how you killed her. You killed her because you were on the trapeze and you were alone. You wanted me up there with you. I never realized how badly you wanted me. It must have been awful, knowing that the only way to get me was by getting rid of Gert. So you put on a pair of gloves and you picked up that ash tray and you killed her. And you had me. You had me up there on the trapeze but once you had me you didn't

237

want me any more. So you threw me away. You told the police Gert said I did it. At the trial you testified cleverly, giving them all the reasons why I would want to kill Gert, drilling it into them that I killed her. They had my fingerprints on the ash tray and they had your story and that was enough for them. And I had nothing. Because I knew nothing. I thought it was an accident that killed her and I didn't know how badly you had wanted me."

"You can't take them back."

"But I can, Madge. The other night when you and Bob were in Irene's apartment you made certain statements and Bob made certain statements and I can take them back with that."

Her gaze drifted past him. She said, "You've got Bob with you."

"He doesn't know it yet, but he's with me. And you're alone. And when I take them back to the day Gert was killed I'll have all of them with me and you'll remain alone. When you come right down to it, Madge, you've always been alone—"

"Give it up, Vincent. Walk away from it. You can't go out selling when you have nothing to sell."

"—because you wanted to be alone. Because whenever you got what you wanted you were anxious to get rid of it. But when you saw someone else get hold of it you couldn't stand that. You knew Irene Janney wanted me and you killed Fellsinger because it was your best way of making sure she'd never get me. You knew they'd give me the chair for the murder of Fellsinger. That was the big thing in your mind when you killed him, when you told yourself

238

you were rid of me once and for all and no one else would have me. It was more important than any other thing, even your practical reasons for killing him."

"Take my advice, Vincent, and give it up. There's no way you can build a case against me."

"You see, Madge? Even now you're still trying to make sure she doesn't get me. You're really a specimen, Madge. It's almost impossible to figure you out. But it just happens bright orange shows up against a dark street."

"That's no evidence. You don't have anything there. What you need is a confession. That's what you're trying to get, isn't it?"

"Well, it would simplify matters, anyway. As things stand now I know what you did, the reasons and the methods. And the problems you faced. Your first real problem came when you knocked on the door of Irene's apartment and then you heard the phonograph going and then you heard me telling you to go away. You had a feeling that wasn't Bob's voice and when you were outside you kept looking at the window. And then you checked up on Bob, and meanwhile you learned I was loose from San Quentin. And here's where you get that Academy Award, because you knew she was interested in me, you had it analyzed from the very beginning, and underneath that mask of an ignorant pest you were laughing at her, because here she was, in there pitching for me and I didn't even know there was such a person as Irene Janney."

"She told you that. She told you to come here."

"No. You're not even warm. I'm the banker now. I've got all of it. I can see you with your problems. I can see you thinking it over, telling yourself I was on the loose, and as long as you knew and I knew I didn't kill Gert, it was possible I'd use my freedom to try and find out who did kill her. Then you were worried about it, you knew you had to do something definite and drastic. There was that very big surprise, that Irene Janney had more brains than you gave her credit for and she was hiding me in her apartment. So you knew you had to begin with keeping an eye on the apartment. Then when I came out you followed me. Your bright orange roadster followed the taxi to Fellsinger's place. You watched when I pressed the button. When I went up you came in and saw Fellsinger's name alongside that particular button. You knew it was only a question of time before the police would visit Fellsinger and ask him if I had tried to make contact. That time element was important. You wanted me to hurry and come down, and when I came down you slipped out from wherever you were hiding and you went in and pressed that same button. You were planning it then, as you went upstairs. And what you wanted most of all was to make sure that Irene Janney would never get me. Next to that you wanted to make sure Fellsinger wouldn't help me find out who killed Gert. Then again you knew if you killed Fellsinger every finger would point at me because the police knew of my friendship with Fellsinger and you were certain they'd find my fingerprints in the room and that was all they needed. So you went in there and killed

Fellsinger. You got talking to him and you got him off guard and you did away with him. Didn't you?"

"Yes."

"Will you tell that to the police?"

"No."

"They'll get it out of you anyway. Because they'll have facts to work with. They'll have that motivation aspect. Don't forget the big item about Bob. He'll be with me."

She smiled. "That's no good. Bob would be recognized as a prejudiced witness. Besides, what could he say? He'd say I wanted you. What tangible proof would he have?"

"A signed statement from the man you hired to follow him. The man who turned right around and played both ends against the middle and followed me to your apartment. That signed statement, Madge, that does it."

She stopped smiling. She said, "All right, that's concrete in itself, but it isn't sufficient. The jealousy factor isn't strong enough."

"Then let's make it stronger. Let's bring in a nasty bit of gossip concerning Bob and Gert."

"Bob. And Gert. Bob and Gert. No. No, don't try that on me. That's not possible."

"But that's the way it is. And when Bob gets up and admits his connection with Gert it bursts the whole thing wide open."

"I'll tell them I never knew anything like that was going on. And I'll be telling the truth."

"They won't believe you, Madge. You hired that man to follow Bob. That's an act of frenzy and it establishes motivation. You're afraid now. And I'll tell you this—as soon as you knew I was here in town you were really scared stiff. Otherwise you would have found a way to tip off the police and let them know I was hiding at Irene Janney's apartment. But you were really scared by that time, whereas before that you were only uncomfortable. And now you couldn't bring the police in on it because you thought Irene Janney and I were working on something and maybe we had it at a point where we were just about ready to hand it over to the police. The only way you could bust that up was to bring in a second killing, to kill Fellsinger. That's where the practical side comes in, but it wasn't practical enough. You overlooked a big issue. If I had facts to prove I hadn't killed Gert, why would I want to kill Fellsinger?"

"You know, I thought of that."

"You thought of it when it was too late. Fellsinger was already dead. You had slipped up on that and maybe you had slipped up on other things, so you were still afraid to give it to the police. The night you came to Irene's place you weren't putting on any act. You were really in bad shape. You were hoping I wouldn't be there and it would mean I had skipped town and I was running away from the whole thing. That was what you wanted, because then you'd know for sure the Fellsinger investment was paying dividends your way, and you could finally talk to the police. But here it comes, trouble again. Irene says Bob will be arriving any minute now and she won't let you hide in the bedroom. So you know I'm in that bedroom. Then you're sick. You're going around on a spinning wheel and you can't get off. What's Vincent Parry up to? What's keeping him here in San Francisco? Why doesn't he run away? What is he waiting for? And how long is he going to wait? I'm afraid—I'm afraid. Right, Madge?"

She ran thin forefingers up and down the creases of the pale orange slacks. She looked at her knees, then she arranged the violet box of candy in the middle of her lap and studied the contents.

Parry folded his arms and watched her.

She selected a chocolate and brought it up slowly toward her mouth and when she had it halfway there she stopped its progress, she let it come into her palm and her hand closed on it and she squeezed it. The chocolate surface broke and white butter cream came gushing out between her fingers. Her head swayed from side to side and she opened her mouth as if in a frantic need for air. She kept squeezing the mashed candy and then all at once snapped her hand open and looked at what she had done. There was a mess of chipped chocolate and butter cream all over her palm and dripping between her fingers. She let out a grinding noise of disgust and rubbed the stuff on her slacks. Then she rubbed her hand on the bright orange house coat, kept rubbing until her hand was clean again. Then she looked at the mess on her slacks and her house coat and she raised her head and her mouth remained open, wide open now in a loose, sagging sort of way.

She said, "I want you, Vincent. At night I've cried in my want for you."

He unfolded his arms and held them stiff, away from his sides.

"All right, Vincent. Let's examine it. She's got you now. She's got you and you've got me. But if you don't hold onto me it means they're still after you. And as long as you don't have me it means you can't prove anything because I won't be there to admit anything. Motivation alone isn't enough. They'll want certain facts."

"You'll be there," he said. He took a few steps backward so that he was between the low rounded chair and the door.

"You're wrong, Vincent. You'll never to able to prove it because I won't be there. You need evidence, you need something concrete, you need a witness. And you don't have a witness, do you? No. Of course you don't."

He watched her. She began to laugh lightly and with enjoyment.

The various shades of orange were merging and melting and flowing toward him.

She kept laughing. She said, "You don't have a witness—no witness."

"I've got the facts and I've got you and that's all I need."

"The facts aren't enough. You can't prove them without me."

"But I've got you."

"No, Vincent. You don't have me." She stood up. She smiled at him.

He said, "Do you think I'm going to stand here and let you get away?"

She took a long breath and he could hear the dragging in her throat. She said, "They'll always be looking for you. She wants you very badly. And that's why she'd be willing to run away with you and keep on running away and always scared, always running away. And it would ruin everything for her but she wouldn't care because she'd be with you and that's all she wants. And you know that and that's why you won't take her. That's why she doesn't have you now and she'll never have you and nobody will ever have you. And that's the way I wanted it. And that's the way it is. And it will always be that way."

She laughed at him and he saw the gold inlays. He saw the bright orange going back and away from him, going too fast. She was running backwards, throwing herself backwards as he went after her but she was too fast and he saw the gold inlays glittering and the bright orange flaring as her arms went wide as the gold inlays flashed as she hit the window and the window gave way and the cracked glass went spraying and she went through.

He was at the window. He leaned through the broken window and he saw her going down, the bright orange acrobat falling off the trapeze. And it was as if she was taking him with her as she went down, the bright orange rolling and tossing and going down and hitting the pavement five stories below. He saw two baby carriages and two women and he heard the women screeching.

Then he saw the upturned faces of the women. And he knew they were staring at the face of the man up there, framed in broken glass. They screeched

245

louder.

He ran out of the apartment, thinking of Irene, darted toward the elevator, thinking of Irene, knew he couldn't use the elevator or the front entrance. He ran down the corridor and took the fire escape. He was thinking of Irene. He used an alley and a narrow street and another alley and finally a street with car tracks. He waited there, thinking of Irene and then a street car came along and took him to the center of town. He ran to the hotel, his brain jammed with Irene. He went up to his room and got into the new clothes and packed his things. Then he was downstairs and paying for one day and saying he was called out of town unexpectedly and he was thinking of Irene and he was seeing her alone in her little apartment and at the window as he went away and wanting him to come back, wanting him to take her with him. And he was trying to tell her how much he wanted to take her with him but he couldn't take her with him because now there was no way to prove his innocence and they would always be running away and even though the road was wide it was dark, frantic, and there was no certainty. There would be a haven now and then but no certainty and he couldn't do that to her. He told himself she was all alone and he would always think of her as all alone and he told himself to go back there and take her with him. He told himself he couldn't do that to her. Here she had a home and she was safe. With him she would never be safe and she would never have a home because a home was never a home when it was a hideaway and he knew what it was to hide and run and hide again.

He couldn't ask her to share that even though he knew she would leap at sharing it. And he knew once she had it, once it hit her, she wouldn't say anything and she would cover up and smile and say everything was all right. That was Irene. That was his girl. That was the happiness, the sweet purity he had always wanted and wanted now more than anything. And he could hear her pleading with him to come back and take her. He could hear himself pleading with himself to go back and take her. And under flashing sunlight the road remained dark.

He walked out of the hotel and kept walking until he found a two-by-four bus depot. He went in and a lot of people in low-priced clothes were sitting on a bench facing a splintered counter. He went up to the counter and a young man behind the counter asked him where he wanted to go and he said Patavilca and the young man said what was that again and he said Arizona and the young man asked where in Arizona and he said Maricopa.

The young man picked up a route map and asked him if he was going alone and he nodded. Then he had his ticket and he found a place on the bench and sat down to wait. It was very warm and sticky in there. He began to think of Arbogast.

They would never know who had done away with Arbogast. They wouldn't even take the trouble to attempt finding out. They had Arbogast listed as a cheap crook and it would be a convenience to cross him off the list. All very quick and automatic, easy to picture. Someone would come across the body and police would identify the body and bury it and say good riddance. But the picture was upside down.

The whole thing was upside down. And the world was spinning in the wrong direction. They had it complete diagnosed. There wasn't a segment of doubt in their minds. This man had killed his wife. And then he had gone ahead and killed his best friend. And then while he was at it he had sought out the woman who had testified against him and he had pushed her through a window.

His lips were building a dim smile. The taxi driver was coming into his mind, along with Coley. He wondered if they were still speaking to each other. Probably, because they couldn't discuss their awful mistake with anyone else. The taxi driver would say it didn't pay to be nice to people. Coley would say there was nothing they could do about it and they might just as well forget about it. And they would never forget about it. They would always feel certain they had helped a killer to kill two more people. He felt sorry for them. He wished there was a way he could straighten them out on that.

Someone said, "Do these buses ever run on schedule?"

A skinny woman with two children on her lap said, "What do they care? You think they're worried about us?"

"That's the way it goes." The someone was a tall man wearing a straw hat. He had a thin mouth that flapped down at the corners. His tie was knotted a good two inches below the collar. "Yes," he said, working his mouth as if there was something sour inside, "it's just one big battle royal all the way

248

through. Nobody gives a hang about the other fellow."

"It's so hot in here," the woman said. The smaller child started to slip away from her lap and she pulled him back and said, "Sit still."

The man sighed. He took off the straw hat, scratched the top of a bald head. "So," he said, gazing at the wall, "that's the way it goes."

"Sometimes," the woman said, "I get tired. I just get sick and tired of everything. Nothing to look forward to."

The man gestured toward the children. "You got them kids," he said. "That's something. Look at me. I got nobody."

"These are my sister's kids," the woman said. "She's been sick and I been caring for them. Now she's all better and I'm taking them back."

"Where?"

"Tucson. Then I'll be coming back here and I'll be alone again. I tell you it aint bearable when a person has nothing to look forward to."

"You mean these aint your kids?"

"I wish they were. Look at them. They're fine little boys."

The man was looking at the woman. The man handled his tie and brought the knot up to the collar. The knot glowed like a lamp far down the dark road.

Parry left the bench and walked out of the bus depot. He was walking fast. He went into a drugstore on the corner and picked up a telephone book. He found the number he wanted and went into the booth and put a nickel in the slot. He dialed and waited while the other phone rang once and then twice and then she said hello.

He said, "It's Allan."

"Where are you? Are you all right?"

"Yes. What are you doing?"

"Just sitting here."

"All right. Listen. It was Madge. But I can't use it. I went up there for a showdown and she did away with herself. Went through the window. You'll read all about it in the afternoon edition. You'll read I pushed her out. I just want you to know I didn't push her out."

"That's not why you called. There's something else you want me to know."

He grinned while tears arrived. He said, "It's nice when you have something to look forward to. Get yourself a map of South America. In Peru there's a little town on the coast. Patavilca. Say it. Tell me where it is."

"Patavilca. In Peru."

"Good. Now listen. I won't write. There can't be any connection whatsoever. And we've got to wait. We've got to give it plenty of time. Maybe they'll get a lead on you and they'll keep an eye on you for a while. Meanwhile if I manage to make it down there I'll be waiting for you. And if you see your way clear—listen to all these ifs."

"We'll skip the ifs," she said. "I get the idea and that's all I require. The general idea. Now hang up on me. Just like that—hang up."

He hung up. He hurried back to the depot and saw the bus gliding into the parking space alongside the waiting room. The passengers formed a jagged line and going into the bus they moved hungrily toward empty seats. Parry found a seat in the rear of the bus and gazing frontward he saw the man in the straw hat sitting next to the skinny woman and the two children sat together across the aisle. The driver came hopping into the bus and closed the door. A few people on the outside were waving good-by. The driver started the motor and then he faced the passengers and he said, "All set?"

TURN TO RICHARD P. HENRICK
FOR THE BEST IN UNDERSEA ACTION!

SILENT WARRIORS   (1675, $3.95)
The RED STAR, Russia's newest, most technically advanced submarine, has been dispatched to spearhead a massive nuclear first strike against the U.S. Cut off from all radio contact, the crew of an American attack sub must engage the deadly enemy alone, or witness the explosive end of the world above!

THE PHOENIX ODYSSEY   (1789, $3.95)
During a routine War Alert drill, all communications to the U.S.S. PHOENIX suddenly and mysteriously vanish. Deaf to orders cancelling the exercise, in six short hours the PHOENIX will unleash its nuclear arsenal against the Russian mainland!

COUNTERFORCE   (2013, $3.95)
In an era of U.S.-Soviet cooperation, a deadly trio of Kremlin war mongers unleashes their ultimate secret weapon: a lone Russian submarine armed with enough nuclear firepower to obliterate the entire U.S. defensive system. As an unsuspecting world races towards the apocalypse, the U.S.S. TRITON must seek out and destroy the undersea killer!

FLIGHT OF THE CONDOR   (2139, $3.95)
America's most advanced defensive surveillance satelllite is abandoning its orbit, leaving the U.S. blind and defenseless to a Soviet missile attack. From the depths of the ocean to the threshold of outer space, the stage is set for mankind's ultimate confrontation with nuclear doom!

WHEN DUTY CALLS   (2256, $3.95)
An awesome new laser defense system will render the U.S.S.R. untouchable in the event of nuclear attack. Faced with total devastation, America's last hope lies onboard a captured Soviet submarine, as U.S. SEAL team Alpha prepares for a daring assault on Russian soil!